The Ascension Legacy

Book 4

A Fallen Hero

Gary Richardson

First originally published by Gary Richardson 2022

ISBN 978-1-7923-9533-8 (Paperback)
ISBN 978-1-7923-9534-5 (Digital)

Printed in the United States of America

Dylon Jr. and Aria, this one is for you two

Gary Richardson

Series Reminders

What follows is a summary reminder of all places, names, and other key identifiers which is
coupled with a pronunciation guide in the previous books. Any places, names, or similar identifiers included in this book will have a similar pronunciation guide, so no fretting. Any new characters, places, or items introduced in this book will not appear in this list but will have an appropriate pronunciation guide in the book near its first appearance to avoid any potential spoilers.

Pronunciation guide:

Rishdel (Rish-del)

Corsallis (Cor-sol-is)

Kirin (Kear-in)

Bjiki (Bee-zee-key)

Mechii (Meh-chi)

Kaufmor (Cough-more)

Norsdin (Nor-sh-den)

Skeel (Scale)

Triandal (Trin-dull)

Izu (Is-ew)

Arissa (Ah-riz-sa)

Leza (Le-z-ah)

Baolba (Bowel-ba)

Derkar (Der-car)

Nefarion (Ne-fair-e-on)

Ailaire (El-air)

Ellias (El-i-us)

Raiken (Rye-ken)

Sagrim (Sag-rim)

Trylon (Try-lawn)

Rhorm (Roar-mm)

Macadre (Ma-cod-dre)

Riorik (Re-or-ick)

Cyrel (Sear-el)

Shadrack (Shad-rack)

Nordahs (Nor-duh-sh)

Nectana (Neck-ta-on-ah)

Heilstur (Hill-st-ur)

Aqutarios (Ah-k-tar-e-os)

Grue (Grew)

Kelig (Kale-ig)

Gromard (Grow-mard)

Tyleco (Tie-le-co)

Do'ricka (Door-ick-ah)

Argrip (Are-grip)

Perigrine (Pair-eh-grin)

Rakish (Rack-ish)

Ami (Ah-me)

Ori (Or-ee)

U'gik (Ew-gick)

Veyron (Vay-ron)

Yorid (Your-id)

Bostic (Boss-tick)

Jayn (Jane)

Droth (Draw-th)

Brem (Brim)

Dylo (Die-low)

Theon (They-on)

Daldon (Dowl-don)

Kerros (Care-o-ss)

Draynard (Dre-nard)

Morthia (More-thigh-ah)

Fielboro (Fail-bore-o)

Asbin (As-bin)

Deaijo (Day-hoe)

Wuffred (Woo-fred)

Brennan (Bren-in)

Dava (Day-va)

Klienheart (K-line-heart)

Via (Vie-ah)

Tanion (Tan-ya-un)   Freca (Freh-ka)

Zox (like "socks" but with a z)   Coway (Cow-way)

Arin (Are-in)   Aurochs (Or-awk-s)

Neddit (Ned-it)   Barbos (Bar-bo-s)

Valstrand (Veil-strand)   Alaricea (Ah-lar-eye-see-ah)

Pan (Pan)   Magnus (Mag-n-us)

Ammudien (Ah-mew-dee-in)   Algon (Al-gone)

Whilem (Will-um)

Chapter 1

The sounds of shouting and struggling could be heard echoing through the thick, dark stone hallways leading to Macadre's throne room. The room was empty, except for its lone occupant who sat perfectly still and upright in his throne, awaiting the incoming prisoner. The floor was dimly lit by the light of several flickering candle flames that cast a variety of shadows, as the three guards drug their captured prize across the floor before stopping before their leader.

Once at the base of the stairs leading up to the stone throne, the guards casually threw the cuffed and chained prisoner to the floor at their feet. It was Tanion, Whilem's dark elf companion. He rested on his hands and knees on the stone floor, as blood dripped from his nose and mouth. It was apparent that his capture and transport had not been free of conflict.

"Sire, we have brought Tanion, as you have ordered," spoke one of the guards standing over the bloodied dark elf.

"So, I see," was their leader's response, as he stood from his gilded throne and walked towards Tanion.

"I also see that you have taken it upon yourselves to start his torture early," he said, as he inspected Tanion's bruised and bloody face.

A wave of fear washed over the guards. They had not been instructed to not harm Tanion, so they took joy in his somewhat violent capture and transport. But now, they were beginning to fear their exuberance might spell their death if their master was unhappy with Tanion's current state of health.

"Our orders were to capture and return the dark elf. There was no mention of a desired condition other than 'alive', so when he resisted, we found it necessary to persuade him otherwise," the guard replied.

Their masked leader only chuckled at the reply before returning to his throne of carved rock.

"I applaud your brutality," he said as he took his seat once more. "And my orders were to simply bring him here. His condition was of little concern, so long as he was breathing enough to answer my questions. You have done well."

The trio of guards bowed at their master's compliment towards their handiwork. Unsure of what to do next, the guards did not say a word, and an awkward silence fell over the room as they waited for their next orders. Their leader only sat in his hewn chair and stared at Tanion. After several seconds, he looked up to see the guards still in the room.

"I see you are still here," he said, somewhat annoyed to the guards.

"We await your orders, Sire," the lead guard answered. "What would you have us do with the prisoner now?"

"You are to do nothing with the prisoner," was the answer they got. "You are to leave my presence immediately and report to your commander. We prepare for war, or have you not heard?"

"Y-y-yes, we have heard of the coming war," answered the guard. "As you wish, my Lord."

The guards turned to walk out of the empty great hall. The third guard gave Tanion a swift kick in the ribs for good measure as he departed from the throne room. Tanion lurched sideways under the force of the blow before spitting up a large amount of blood. From beneath his mask, the dark elf's captor smiled Tanion's misfortune.

Eventually, Tanion was able to position himself so that he sat on the floor on his knees with his cuffed hands resting in his lap. He stared at his masked captor, as the armor-clad individual stared back at him.

The punishment for betrayal was death, so Macadre's leader's impulse was to do what he had done many times before to those he suspected of working against him—remove his shining sword from its sheath before removing the heads of his victims from their shoulders. But, this time was different. This time, Tanion had information that he needed before any such punishment could be rendered. Now was the time for talking, not killing.

"Tell me, what business did Whilem have with the bird keeper before you killed him?" he asked Tanion.

"What bird keeper?" Tanion asked defiantly.

The dark elf's refusal amused the mysterious leader, who laughed at his captive's attempt to rebel.

"I had hoped that you would give me reason to torture you," the hidden captor said slyly, as he slowly drew his sword from its resting place.

In the dimly lit throne room, the sword began to emit the eerily faint blue glow that had inspired fear in so many others before.

"Now, shall we try this again?" the unseen king asked.

"Or what, you'll kill me?" replied Tanion, still with a defiant tone.

"Heavens no," was his captor's answer. "You are of no value to me dead. At least not right now. Instead, I think I have another plan."

He stepped behind the seated dark elf and gave him a hard kick in the back. The blow knocked Tanion forward onto all fours. However, before Tanion could recover, the armored leader placed his steel-plated boot firmly on Tanion's hand, pinning it to the floor with all the dark elf's fingers splayed out. Unable to free himself, Tanion had no choice but to let the scene play out according to his captor's will.

The dominant king slowly lowered the tip of his sword so that it rested on Tanion's pinky finger. He slid the sword's tip along the finger until it reached the knuckle, just before the dark elf's ragged fingernail. Then, he slowly pushed the sword under the knuckle. The razor-sharp blade easily sliced through the skin as it made its way beneath the finger, and blood ran down the blade onto the floor beneath. Once in position, with a simple flick of his wrist, the glowing blade lopped off the tip of Tanion's pinky and sent the dismembered appendage flying across the empty room. Tanion cried out in pain despite his best attempt not to.

"Now, shall I repeat the question again or will you tell me what I seek to know?" the self-appointed king asked, as he moved his sword to the middle knuckle of Tanion's pinky finger.

"Whilem had no business with the old man. His death was an unfortunate accident," Tanion answered between his heavy breaths, as he tried to fight off the pain.

His answer was not accepted.

Another flick of the wrist, and another piece of Tanion's little finger flew across the great hall. The dark elf cried out in pain once more. And the sword tip moved up to the last joint of Tanion's finger, as his pinned hand now sat in a pool of his own blood.

"All right, all right," Tanion cried out. "I killed the bird keeper. It had nothing to do with Whilem though. The old man made disparaging comments about my family, so I killed him out of honor."

"Wrong!" shouted his torturer.

A third flick of the wrist sent the last part of Tanion's pinky finger flipping through the air. And as before, Tanion cried out in pain. The sword's action was swift, but nonetheless, the severing of his digit caused a great amount of searing pain throughout the dark elf's entire body. His hand throbbed horribly, as a steady stream of blood spurted from the place where his finger once sat.

"You have nine more fingers left, Tanion. How many do you want to leave here with? The choice is yours, but I am prepared to keep asking the question until all of them are gone."

The sword then scraped across the ground as it moved towards the first knuckle of Tanion's next finger.

"Okay! Okay! Okay!" Tanion shouted. "I'll talk. I'll talk. Just put the sword away."

But the sword was not put away. It remained positioned under Tanion's ring finger as it slightly bobbed up and down waiting for the dark elf to talk.

"When I get the information I seek, the sword will be sheathed," came the reply from Tanion's captor.

"All right, fine. Whilem had the bird keeper send a message to some bandits near Tyleco who had frequented his tavern in the past. He wanted them to disrupt the gnolls you had sent and return some item to him," cried Tanion.

"And why would he do that?" the king of the North asked.

"His sister was killed outside of Barbos by some orcs—your orcs—so he wanted revenge for her death," was Tanion's next answer.

The dark elf's answer confused his captor. There was no reason for the gnolls and orcs he dispatched to have gone as far as Barbos. Luckily for him, his masked covered the perplexed expression on his face. Immediately, his thoughts began racing as he tried to make sense of this information.

"Did Kelig send my troops to Barbos as part of a trap? Could Kelig be in cahoots with Whilem to send Grue on a wild goose chase while he and Whilem conspired to take what is mine?"

The more he thought about it the more it did not seem logical, given Whilem's mission to have the bandits near Tyleco attack some of his troops and 'return some item to him'. It still did not answer why at least some of his troops were near Barbos. This made him think that Whilem's motivation was just another lie, either from Whilem to Tanion or just from Tanion to him. Regardless, Whilem's motives were of little consequence now that his goal was revealed.

"Hmm. That is most interesting," the armored leader said, as he tried to hide the questions that still rumbled through his mind. "And why would you opt to help Whilem in this endeavor, knowing that traitors receive death here?"

Tanion's response was immediate and telling.

"My parents once stood up to you when you commandeered their farm just outside Nectana for your troops several years ago. I was only a teenager, but you made me watch as you forced my father to watch your gnolls eat my mother alive, and then I had to watch as you slowly dismembered my father. Whilem took me in and cared for me after you destroyed my family, so I felt obligated to help him, especially if it meant striking back at you."

"And now? Do you still think it wise to defy me as your parents did?" Tanion's torturer asked as he lifted his boot from Tanion's hand, releasing the dark elf.

Tanion sat up and quickly covered the still profusely bleeding appendage.

"No, Sire, I do not. I was wrong to conspire against you. Your will is the only will worth serving," the wounded dark elf cried out, desperate to save his life and ease his suffering.

"So, are you ready to abandon your flawed loyalty to that traitor Whilem and truly serve my kingdom?"

"Yes. Yes, I will only serve you!" shouted Tanion.

"Excellent," the masked leader replied, as he turned and moved a few steps towards the great hall's main exit.

"Guards," he called out to get the attention of the two armored guards that stood watch at the entrance.

The two guards came quickly marching into the great hall and to their commander-in-chief, who had returned to Tanion's side.

"Yes, my Lord, how may we be of service?" asked one of the guards, as they both bowed before their feared leader.

"We have a new recruit. Tanion here has realized that it is better to serve me than defy me. Take him to be fitted and equipped for our upcoming battle," their leader demanded.

The guards lifted Tanion to his feet. They spun the wounded elf around and began to lead him from the room.

But, after only a few steps, Tanion's journey ended abruptly.

"No traitor shall be given the chance to betray a second time," the leader exclaimed before he shoved his sword through Tanion's back and out his chest. Blood ran from Tanion's mouth and down his chin as his eyes slowly closed before dying.

"Toss this traitor's body on the floor of Whilem's tavern, and let it be known that any who defy me will suffer a similar fate," came the orders to the guards from their leader.

The guards drug Tanion's body across the floor, leaving a trail of blood in its wake, as they set about completing their newly issued mission.

***

As morning dawned over the decimated bandit camp, Wuffred and Ammudien decided it was time to put the gnome's plan to recover the Shield of Sagrim from the guardhouse in Tyleco into action. They had determined that the best course of action would be to have Wuffred return to the Tyleco gate and ask to speak with the guard captain, who had previously warned Wuffred not to return to Tyleco unannounced. Their assumption was that the guards would escort Wuffred back into the guardhouse where he would meet and talk with Captain Cooper, and when that happened, an invisible Ammudien would sneak into the guardhouse and into the room where Wuffred had seen the shield, and the gnome would then steal the relic and wait to follow Wuffred out of the guardhouse once his conversation with the captain had concluded. With time of the essence, the pair opted to start as early in the day as possible, so they could return with the precious item and continue their quest.

"Right," started Ammudien. "Once I cast this spell, I can maintain it indefinitely, but it requires a great deal of focus and concentration. And, I will not be able to cast any other magic without disrupting my invisibility, so I will be totally defenseless if our ruse is detected or Wuffred finds himself in danger."

The others nodded along with Ammudien's words, as he had repeated them several times since the plans inception. His warning was nothing new to the group, but it was the gnome's only method of conveying his deep concerns for his own safety inside the human town.

Riorik, who was starting to improve from the poison's effects and could now sit upright on his own, and Nordahs began offering their words of confidence regarding the pair's assured success. Ammudien thanked the two elves for their support, but Wuffred seemed not to notice their words. The berserker was preoccupied in his search for Asbin, who was not to be found with the group. His head was on a swivel, as he looked across the tower's floor and outside the tower's entrance for his beloved Asbin.

After a few minutes, a pale Asbin returned to the tower, wiping her chin with the back of her hand. Wuffred looked at her curiously, but Ammudien could tell that she had been outside vomiting, just as she had the day before, when the group searched the bandits for money so Wuffred could buy the ingredients to cure Riorik's poisonous wound.

"Are you all right, my dear?" a concerned Wuffred asked Asbin.

"Yes, yes. I'm fine, just not feeling well this morning," she replied, as she gently patted Wuffred's chest with her clean hand.

"She says she has been ill the past few days, but I theorized that her contact with Riorik's ailment may be exacerbating her current illness. She insists that I am wrong though," a suspicious Ammudien added to the conversation.

"Is this true?" the berserker asked, still obviously very concerned about the person of his most intimate desires.

Asbin nodded, confirming Ammudien's previous assertion about her pre-existing condition.

"It is," she answered, "but it generally fades as the day goes on, and I'm fine."

Asbin clearly knew the signs she was exhibiting were that of a pregnancy, but her naïve companions were so focused on their own quests that they remained clueless about the true nature of her condition, so she chose to keep it a secret. Plus, if she were pregnant, it could only mean one thing; she was carrying Wuffred's child. The pair had been careful to keep their romance a secret up to this point, but that did not mean the two had not managed to sneak some intimacy into their relationship along the way.

She was scared by the prospect of carrying a berserker's child within her womb. There had never been any records of a dwarf ever bearing a child of a berserker. There was no way to know how dangerous it could be to Asbin during the pregnancy, what effect it may have on the child during the pregnancy or after its birth, or how such a prospect would be viewed by those around her, especially her friends that now depended on her as much as she did them. Would her condition be accepted by her friends, would the child be accepted by society or labeled a monster and deemed unworthy of life, and would Wuffred accept the child? Her head was full of fears, and she was not ready to confront them today.

In fact, when Asbin first realized that she had conceived, the dwarf contemplated brewing and consuming a potion that would expel the growing life from her womb. However, the gentle healer was disgusted at the thought of such an act and quickly decided against it. This was not just her child, she thought, so it was not just her decision. It was one that she felt required Wuffred's input as well, but she was afraid to discuss it with him given the newness of their relationship. That fear remained with her, as she was still unprepared to mention it to her half-human lover, especially before his departure on such a risky mission.

"How long has this been going on?" asked Wuffred, who along with the others was curious to know more about Asbin's so-called illness.

"Only for a few days now," she replied, "but like I said, it is mainly only in the mornings and I'm better as the day goes on. I haven't said anything because we were so close to the temple that I did not want to distract from our quest. And, I would like to think that my actions the past few days will speak for themselves in showing that my condition has not negatively impacted my ability to perform my role in our group."

That last bit she added with somewhat of a stern and angry tone in her voice, to both persuade the others that she was not debilitated by her condition in any way and to dissuade them from questioning her further on the matter. Her plan seemed to work as the others all nodded and shrugged in agreement that she still seemed more than capable even if she was ill, so nobody chose to press the subject more.

"Now," she continued, "if nobody has anything else to say about my condition, I need to see to Riorik's wound again if he hopes to be healed in time to move on once you two return."

She walked towards Riorik and somewhat roughly hoisted his tunic to reveal his back. It was not her usual delicate and caring approach as her frustration and fear of her current state was emotionally overwhelming.

Riorik winced at the burning sensation from his clothing rubbing against the still sensitive areas of his back. The discoloration had receded and no longer covered the whole of his back. The concoction Asbin had made from the ingredients Wuffred procured in Tyleco was obviously working, as it drew the poison from the elf's body and secreted it out of his pores in the form of dark, almost opaque, sweat. By applying the sloppy ointment to the affected areas every few hours, Asbin had dramatically reduced the poison's infection and had allowed Riorik to improve dramatically. It would only take a few more applications of the healer's medicine to completely rid the ranger of the poison and its dastardly purpose.

Asbin's fears and frustration subsided as she looked at the fruits of her labor. She knew that her efforts would not only keep Riorik alive but would eventually remove even the slightest sign of the poison's presence from his slender body. A small smile of satisfaction spread across her lips, as she dipped her hand into the pouch the held the remaining ointment before she set about rubbing the greasy solution into Riorik's skin. The amount of ointment needed decreased with each use, and now with the discoloration isolated to the small of Riorik's back, she knew that it would only require another one or two applications before he would be fully healed. The dwarf expected that Riorik would be rid of the poison before Wuffred and Ammudien returned, so it would only be a matter of how the elf's stamina recovered, something that her ointment could not help. But, seeing Riorik sitting upright and talking was a great improvement from the feeble elf she had seen the day before, so she was encouraged by the speed of his recovery so far.

"There you go," she told Riorik, as she gently lowered his tunic back down. "Another treatment or two and you should be as good as new."

Having calmed down, she walked away from Riorik and back to Wuffred. Her head barely reached the bottom of his ribs. She threw her arms around one of Wuffred's thighs; they were too short to reach all the way around his larger frame. Her head was buried in his side, as she squeezed him in a loving embrace.

"You be careful today," she told Wuffred.

"And you," she said as she pushed her head back and stared at Ammudien, "do not let anything happen to him unless you want to see what an angry dwarf can do to you while you sleep."

Now, she stepped away from Wuffred and stood in front of the two.

"I expect both of you back here in one piece by nightfall. Do I make myself clear?"

"Yes, ma'am," they both answered as if they were addressing their mother.

The group finished their farewells, and Ammudien set about casting his invisibility spell. With his wand in hand, the gnome began drawing runes in the air as he had done many times before. This time, however, was slightly different. He did not draw the runes in a straight line but rather drew them in a circle around himself and higher up in the air so that they hung above his head. Once the circle was complete, he placed his wand on top of the glowing white runes and pushed them down towards the ground. As the runes passed over Ammudien's body, the gnome began to disappear. Once the runes faded into the ground, the gnome was completely invisible to the onlookers, who stared in amazement.

"Shall we go?" was the question asked in Ammudien's voice from the space now devoid of any visible sign of the gnome's presence.

Wuffred simply nodded before he gave a wink to Asbin, as he turned and headed off towards Tyleco once again. Ammudien, even though nobody could tell, followed closely behind his larger friend.

***

As Wuffred approached the gate outside Tyleco, one of the guards who had witnessed Captain Cooper's warning to Wuffred recognized the advancing berserker. The guard quickly moved to intercept Wuffred and held his pike out to block his path forward.

"You there," the guard shouted in Wuffred's direction. "Captain Cooper was very clear that you were not to return here."

"Actually," Wuffred replied, "he said I was not to return unannounced. And, I am here to announce myself so that I may speak with Captain Cooper. Can you please take me to him?"

"Captain Cooper is not available, so I suggest you move along."

The guard's response was concerning to Wuffred but even more so to the invisible gnome standing in his shadow. The whole plan rested on Wuffred gaining access to the guardhouse so that he could show Ammudien where he had previously spied the relic shield. If this guard refused Wuffred's request, then the group would need to come up with another plan to gain access to the missing armor.

But Wuffred was not willing to give up on his mission just yet.

"Well, is there someplace that I can wait for him?" Wuffred asked. "Thanks to Captain Cooper's help, I was able to return to my family in time to help my sister, and I would just like to express my gratitude for his assistance."

The guard looked at Wuffred with an expression of obvious skepticism at Wuffred's story. Wuffred immediately saw how one might suspect his story to be a simple cover to disguise malevolent intentions. And Wuffred was right, the guard more suspected that Wuffred had not been successful in helping his sister and now sought an audience with Captain Cooper, who he blamed for his sister's death, so that he might inflict harm on the captain.

Wuffred thought he could diffuse the situation in advance.

"I mean no ill will or harm to Captain Cooper, only to say thank you. I am unarmed, and only bring with me a small token of our appreciation in the form of what coin we have remaining. See," he said, as he held out the small coin-filled leather pouch for the guard to inspect.

The guard felt the pouch and was quick to realize that it was indeed just coin as Wuffred claimed. Satisfied the pouch held no threat, the guard gave Wuffred a quick pat down to verify that he was unarmed. The guard found no weapons or other items that could be dangerous in Wuffred's possession. He started to second-guess his earlier assumptions about Wuffred's intentions and slowly began to think that maybe there was some truth to the berserker's request.

After some contemplation, the guard relented.

"Captain Cooper is attending the Security Council briefing with Lord Veyron to discuss the recent gnoll sightings and attacks. You can wait for him in the guardhouse and nowhere else. Once he returns from his meeting, he will see you, but only if he chooses to do so. If he refuses your request, then you will be forcefully removed from our town. Will you agree to these terms?"

"I gladly agree to those terms," Wuffred answered.

This was exactly what the group had hoped for with their plan, so Wuffred would have agreed to pretty much anything if it meant getting him and Ammudien inside the guardhouse.

"Very well then," said the guard. "Wait here while I find a suitable escort to take you to the guardhouse. I cannot allow you to wander the streets on your own."

Wuffred simply nodded to signal his willingness to comply with the guard's plan.

The guard turned to another guard still standing by the gate.

"Send a runner to the barracks. We need someone to take this outsider to the guardhouse so that he may speak to our captain, once he returns from his meeting."

Wuffred stood and stared at the guards for the next several minutes while they all waited for the escort to arrive. He attempted to make small talk with the guard several times, but the guard only answered with brief responses and was unwilling to engage in any conversation with Wuffred.

He had hoped to get the guard talking to provide cover for Ammudien's sounds. The gnome was invisible but not completely silent. Small yawns, the occasional shuffling of bored, impatient feet on the ground, and the sound of his robe sleeves rubbing against his torso could be heard by those nearby, so Wuffred was wanting to distract from the noises and perhaps mask the gnome's noises through casual banter.

"So, there have been other gnoll attacks?" Wuffred asked casually, pretending not to know as much on the subject as he really did.

"I am not at liberty to discuss such matters with you," the guard replied harshly.

Wuffred tried again.

"Well, what of the weather in Tyleco this time of year? Is it always this nice?" the berserker asked.

"The rains have not come yet but are expected soon," was all the guard was willing to say on the topic.

Wuffred's attempts at banter with the guard were failing miserably. But, the awkward exchange was soon interrupted when another guard approached.

"I'm told there is someone here in need of an escort?" the new guard asked the other.

"Yes. This young man has requested to speak with Captain Cooper. The two have met before. Please escort him to the guardhouse, where he is to remain until Captain Cooper either sees him or issues other orders on what is to be done with him."

The escort gave a quick salute to the other guard, who obviously held the higher position within the guard ranks and then motioned for Wuffred to walk ahead of him. Wuffred discreetly motioned for Ammudien to stick close to him, as the pair stepped in front of the escort before walking through the city gate.

Concerned that Ammudien may be kicked or otherwise detected by their escort who walked near, Wuffred thought it wise to change up the order in which they moved.

"Pardon me, sir, but would it be possible for me to follow you? I have only visited this town once before, and I am not entirely certain in what direction I should go," Wuffred offered to his escort.

The request annoyed the guard escort slightly, but if true, then Wuffred was only going to be more of a hindrance in the lead position.

"Well," the escort started, "I would be a fool to walk in front with my back to you. You would only run off, and then what? No, I shan't be so foolish again. But I will walk alongside you as to guide you to your destination."

Wuffred did not know what he meant by being 'so foolish again', but he surmised that it had something to with a previous escort going bad and someone escaping. Regardless, Wuffred achieved his main objective—he got the guard to walk in front of Ammudien, allowing the magically cloaked gnome to walk without fear of being stepped on by their former pursuer.

A short walk later, the trio arrived at the guardhouse. The escort opened the door and nudged Wuffred's shoulder to imply that he was to enter first, but Wuffred remained still. This delay in the berserker's action was to allow the invisible mage ample opportunity to enter the door and clear the doorway so that the others could walk through unimpeded.

After a few seconds, Wuffred heard a soft tapping from just inside the doorway. He took this as a sign from Ammudien that it was safe to enter, so Wuffred casually stepped through the entrance and into the guardhouse with his escort following closely behind. Ammudien hugged the wall allowing the two humans to pass by so that he could once again follow them on their path. Wuffred, now in the lead position again, walked through the hallway towards the waiting room that he visited before. The thought of sitting on that hard rock bench for an untold amount of time was most unpleasant to Wuffred, but it was the only path he knew that led past their goal.

As the group approached the room with the shield, Wuffred stopped just past the doorway making sure that he and his escort did not block Ammudien's entrance to the room. Wuffred spun around and looked at the guard.

"I marveled at that shield the last time I was here. Captain Cooper said something about it being part of Lord Veyron's birthright. Would it be possible for me to take a closer look at it?" Wuffred asked rhetorically.

He knew very well that the guard would not let him see the shield, but he wanted to ask the question aloud so that Ammudien would know that was the room which held their prize. Wuffred felt it too risky to signal the hidden gnome in any other way with the guard so close behind him, so he opted for a less discreet signal.

Discreet or not, it worked. Ammudien understood Wuffred's message and quickly slipped into the room so that he could begin scoping out the room and the case that housed Sagrim's Shield.

"No, you may not get a closer look!" shouted the guard to Wuffred's question. "You are here to speak with the captain and nothing more. If you have designs to steal Lord Veyron's prize, then you will be sorely disappointed because I have my eyes on you."

"Now move it," the guard demanded as he shoved Wuffred away from the armory's door.

Wuffred's task was complete, so there was little reason not to comply. The berserker apologized to the guard, saying that his request was out of line as he continued down the hall and back to the room he had sat in before.

"This is where I met with the captain last time," Wuffred said as he indicated to the room. "Do you suppose it is possible for me to just wait here again?"

Wuffred did not really want to wait on the uncomfortable bench again, but he wanted to stay as close to Ammudien as he could, just in case there was trouble and the gnome needed his help.

"Aye, that is fine," answered the guard. "I suppose I could watch you here just as well as I could somewhere else."

Wuffred took a seat on the rock bench, and his back immediately began to ache just from the memory of his last experience there. The escort stood in the doorway facing

Wuffred, keeping a close eye on the outsider at all times. There was nothing left to do now but wait. Wait and hope that Ammudien could get his hands on the relic that the pair has risked so much to be so close to.

Chapter 2

"Have you come to tell me that my troops are ready to march?" the impatient king asked the messenger that approached his throne.

"No, my Lord," the messenger answered. "But I do bring a message from your agent."

The messenger fell to one knee, as he bowed his head before his leader. He stretched out his hands above his bowed head and held aloft a rolled piece of parchment.

The curious king stood from his carved throne and approached the kneeling messenger. He took the scroll from the messenger's hands and wasted no time in reading its contents.

"My Lord,

You sent word that I was to return to your side in Macadre, but your mission is best served instead by you joining me at the oasis nearest the border of the Narsdin and Heilstur regions. I have located the next piece of armor that you seek, and it is here. I dare not recover it for myself but gladly offer its location to you, as it will surely aid you in whatever acts are to come.

Your faithful servant,

-K"

The message could not have come at a better time. The mysterious king had already planned to stage his invasion at the oasis, and now he received word that another piece of the armor had been found at the same location. His agent had not been told of the plan to meet there, so there could not be any other explanation aside from a miraculous coincidence. The news filled the disguised leader with joy and excitement. He felt his conquest of Corsallis was now closer at hand than previously thought.

"If my troops are not ready now, then how much longer must I be forced to wait?" he angrily asked the still kneeling messenger.

"They are finishing their preparations now, my Lord. They should be ready to march within the next two days," was the answer returned.

"That is too long to wait now," replied the masked dictator. "Ready my horse. I leave for the oasis now. Tell the troops to depart no later than tomorrow. We rendezvous at the oasis as planned."

"Yes, my Lord. And is there a reply you would like sent to this most recent message?" the dutiful messenger asked.

"Yes. Make it known that I make my way to the oasis and that my presence there should be expected soon."

"As you wish, my Lord," answered the messenger before standing up but being careful not to look up at the faceplate that covered his master's face.

Once standing, the messenger turned around, quickly walked out of the great hall, and set about completing the orders he had been given, starting with fetching his master's horse.

Within just a few minutes, another messenger entered the room and announced that the king's horse had been readied and awaited its rider. The dark king did not hesitate to mount his steed before setting off on the long ride across Narsdin, from his palace in Macadre to the oasis near his land's southern border. It would require him to ride through the night at least once, and depending on the weather in the mountain pass, maybe more.

***

Alone in the armory, Ammudien looked around. There were no guards posted in the room, which at first Ammudien thought was odd, but then he remembered that he was in the middle of the guardhouse. There was no need to guard the items in the room from themselves, and the guards were very loyal to Lord Veyron, so none would dare to steal his personal property.

Still, it all seemed too easy to the gnome. He continued to look around the room for traps, alarms, or any other devices that might spoil his efforts going forward. Ammudien spent the next several minutes carefully inspecting the room and especially the glass case that housed the shield but found no sign of anything that would prevent his pending theft from being successful.

Finally convinced that the shield was not rigged or booby-trapped, Ammudien decided it was now or never if he was going to steal the relic. He had no way of knowing how much time he would have in the armory before a guard came in or before Wuffred's ruse came to an end, so this heist was something that needed to be completed sooner rather than later.

The invisible gnome mage made his way behind the pedestal the case sat on. The pedestal itself was as tall as the gnome. This presented a new problem to the logic-oriented mage, who had failed to really notice the height difference during his previous inspection. Ammudien had stood on his invisible tiptoes to look inside the glass for any traps or alarms but was so focused on his search that he remained oblivious to the pedestal's height compared to his own.

Ammudien quickly looked around the room for anything he could stand on to get to a better, higher position that would allow him to do what he came for. It did not take long for him to spy several boxes of arrows stacked up in the room's far corner. The gnome immediately knew that was the solution he sought. The boxes were tall enough that it would only take one or two for him to achieve the desired height and that the contents of the boxes would be light enough that his small frame would be able to relatively easily move them about.

It would have been quite a sight for anyone who looked in the room as Ammudien set about repositioning the needed boxes behind the pedestal. While he was invisible, the boxes were not. The boxes of arrows appeared to float through the air as they were moved by an unseen force from one place in the room to another. The truth was that Ammudien was simply picking up the boxes and carrying them to where he wanted, but his invisibility spell did not extend beyond himself or anything he possessed inside the circle of runes when the spell was cast.

It was only now that Ammudien realized the true flaw in his plan.

The plan had been for Ammudien to remain invisible throughout the ordeal, but in the excitement, he had forgotten that he would have no means to hide the shield once it was acquired. His body, his clothing, and even his backpack had been part of the invisibility spell, so they were all invisible along with their contents, but the shield was not part of it, so no matter where he stashed the shield it would be visible. Even if he stuffed the shield into his backpack, the shield would remain visible to any onlookers. The spell's effect would not extend to anything outside of the spell's original target.

This meant that if Ammudien wanted any chance at exiting Tyleco undetected, then he would have to lift his invisibility only to cast it again so that this time he could include Sagrim's Shield in the effect. This was not a pleasing thought to the gnome, as the spell took some time to cast and would leave him visible and vulnerable until it was completed. But, he knew that he had little other choice and that this approach was better than the alternatives.

However, he wisely decided to remain invisible himself until he had acquired the shield. The less time he spent visible among the humans the safer he was.

With the arrow boxes in place, the still invisible mage carefully climbed the boxes and positioned himself directly behind the glass case. He first looked to see if the case was hinged so that he could simply open the case and withdraw the shield, but no hinges could be found. This indicated to the gnome that the case was little more than a glass lid, which simply needed to be lifted off its base to expose the contents it held within.

He gingerly placed his hands on the sides of the glass case lid and began to slowly lift it from the base. Ammudien had only managed to lift the lid a few inches when he heard the approaching footsteps of someone walking down the hallway. The mage froze in place, still holding the case slightly above its base, hoping that the approaching individual would not notice.

Ammudien nervously watched the doorway as a man in shiny armor strolled past without so much as a pause in front of the armory entrance. The gnome remained perfectly still as he listened to the fading footsteps in the distance, trying to be sure that no other guards might interrupt him again. The hallway fell silent once more, and Ammudien continued.

The mage lifted the lid off the base and carefully climbed down from his makeshift stool before sitting the lid on the ground at the base of the pedestal. With the shield exposed, Ammudien made quick work of pulling the shield from the stand that it sat on. He quickly placed the shield on the ground, leaning it against the wall while he looked for another shield to take its place. A missing shield would be more noticeable than a different shield, so Ammudien planned to replace Sagrim's Shield with a decoy, but there was a problem with this plan too.

Ammudien found a shield but soon discovered that it would not fit in the case. Sagrim's Shield was designed for a gnome, so it was of a much smaller size than the other shields typically carried by the human guards.

Afraid to spend too much time on this issue, Ammudien quickly settled on leaving the case empty. It was more important that he recast his invisibility spell so that he and the shield could discreetly leave the town than it was to have a fitting decoy in the case. The theft would be discovered eventually either way, so his ability to escape with the shield was the obvious priority.

With the decision made to abandon the notion of a decoy, Ammudien quickly placed the lid back on the case atop the pedestal. The least amount of changes would likely result in a slower detection he surmised. Then, he grabbed the shield from its resting place and moved as far back into the room and away from the door as he could. To put the shield under his invisibility spell's effect, it would require him to shed himself of the current spell first, so he wanted to hide from view as much as possible until the new spell was cast.

From under his invisible sleeve, he removed his wand. It was still invisible too at this point, and he began drawing a single rune in the air. The rune hung in the air, glowing orange. With the rune complete, Ammudien walked into the floating symbol. As soon as the rune touched the gnome's robes, the invisibility cloak that had surrounded him dissipated. He was free to cast the spell again and this time include his prize.

He hooked the shield to his backpack like how he had seen Asbin carry hers before tossing the pack over his now visible shoulders. Working quickly, he began casting the same runes that he had cast at the bandit camp earlier that morning. He worked in a circle, just as he had before, until the runes encircled him. And just as before, he dragged the runes down from above his head to the floor of the room. His body, clothes, and possessions faded as the runes passed over them until there was nothing left of the mage to be seen. Ammudien was invisible once more and ready to leave, but first, he had to wait for Wuffred.

***

After a short wait, but what seemed like hours to Wuffred sitting on the hard and rough-cut bench, Captain Cooper finally arrived to speak with his visitor. The guard moved aside, as the captain strolled into the room and stood at its entrance staring at Wuffred.

"I see you have returned. This is most unexpected. Explain yourself," the captain demanded.

Wuffred stood from his seated position to show respect to the captain as he answered.

"I only wished to return and express my sincerest gratitude to you for your leniency and understanding of my family's situation. You could have easily imprisoned me, or at the very least, confiscated my goods, but you did neither. And, thanks to that act of kindness on your behalf, I was able to return to my mother and sister in time to see my sister's wounds healed. Her strength has not yet fully returned, but she improves with each breath. I returned to Tyleco to offer a token of our gratitude," Wuffred told him, as he extended his arm with a small coin purse in his palm.

"It is all we have left, but we owe it to you for helping me save my sister's life," Wuffred added.

Captain Cooper looked at Wuffred and at the coin purse being offered. Captain Cooper, while deeply motivated to improve his position within the ranks of the city's political landscape, was not keen on the idea of accepting money from citizens. Some might see it as him accepting bribes, while others might see it as the act of a callous man who is content to take all that someone else has when obviously their needs are greater than his own. Most people saw his common refusals to accept such rewards as the act of a noble man, but in truth, it was merely a publicity stunt to further his image of a noble man so that he may profit politically, which, as it turned out, was also more rewarding monetarily.

This did not mean that Captain Cooper was a scrupulous man or a deceitful man, only a man that understood public image was not something that could easily be purchased but could be cheaply ruined by a few simple acts observed by the wrong people. He strived to use his position to protect and serve the people of Tyleco and Lord Veyron, so while others pursued coin through whatever means to improve their personal holdings, Captain Cooper used his position politically to help those in need. He also just happened to reap the financial benefits of such a high standing within the city's society.

"I cannot accept such a generous offer," the guard captain replied, as he pushed Wuffred's hand away. "As the captain of Lord Veyron's guard, it is my duty to protect the people of Tyleco. After speaking with you, I did not feel that you were a threat to anyone within these walls and believed that you legally purchased the items found in your possession. As such, I did what any of my guards would have been expected to do—I released you to return to your family. No additional reward is necessary for doing one's job."

The captain did not say it, but he was still somewhat skeptical of Wuffred's tale of woes as the result of a gnoll ambush only to be rescued by elves. There were many things in Wuffred's story that seemed to be corroborated by his attire and the recent reports of gnoll activity outside the city, but something still did not ring true to the captain's ears. And, given the stern warning, the captain had given Wuffred before, it seemed odd that the outsider would return for no other reason than to say thanks, at the risk of punishment or imprisonment.

"I insist," said Wuffred, as he once again extended his hand offering the coin purse.

Wuffred's insistence on the subject raised a red flag in the experienced guard captain's mind. Trained to always be on guard and skeptical of all things, Captain Cooper took Wuffred's assertive behavior as a possible trap. He wondered if perhaps the coin purse held something more than just coins. Maybe Wuffred was lying about his sister's recovery and was here seeking vengeance for her death, which he blamed Captain Cooper for.

Unsure of the truth behind Wuffred's offering, Captain Cooper decided it best to not accept the coin purse but to also not allow Wuffred to linger in the guardhouse any longer.

"If this outsider means me or the other guards harm, then it is best to remove him from our home quickly," Captain Cooper thought to himself before addressing Wuffred one more time.

"Again, I cannot accept your gift," he replied to Wuffred, as he pushed Wuffred's hand away one more time, careful to only touch Wuffred's hand and not the suspect coin purse.

"But," he continued, "I am relieved to hear of your sister's speedy recovery and I do not wish to keep you from her any longer. Please allow my man here to escort you back to the city gate so that you can return to your family. I hope that I do not dishonor you with my refusal but only wish to see that coin put to better use, supporting your family in their time of need instead of only filling my pockets."

He had hoped his answer was enough to defuse any possible situation with Wuffred long enough for him to leave the room, while still being politically correct enough to maintain his public image with the watching guard.

"I really must be going now, so if you will excuse me, I'll be on my way," Captain Cooper told Wuffred as an excuse for his departure and to effectively end this rather suspicious meeting.

Nevertheless, the guard captain was sure to stay ready in case Wuffred made any aggressive moves as he backed away from the outsider and turned to walk out of the room. Wuffred, anxious to leave the city himself, made no such move and was hopeful that he had stalled long enough for Ammudien to have completed his task too.

"No dishonor felt here, Captain Cooper," Wuffred offered to the retreating guard captain.

"Thank you for taking the time to see me and for your kind words," he shouted down the hallway to Captain Cooper, as he walked back towards the guardhouse's entrance and past the armory, with his new escort right behind.

As he walked past the entrance, Wuffred heard a soft whistle, much like a bird call. It was the sign he and Ammudien had agreed on for the gnome to give if he was successful in retrieving the shield. Wuffred was relieved to hear the melodic sound from his hidden companion.

Wuffred increased his pace ever so slightly, knowing that Ammudien had the shield and was following him and his escort. If Ammudien had the shield, then that meant there was a risk that its disappearance could be detected at any moment, and he wanted to be certain the pair of them were as far from the city of Tyleco as possible by the time that happened.

The guard, distracted by his own thoughts of what he could do with the money in Wuffred's coin purse that his captain had refused, barely noticed Wuffred's faster pace. The guard even contemplated taking the coin from Wuffred but quickly thought better of it, given Captain Cooper's seemingly endearing position towards the lad and his wounded sister. If he were to steal it from the outsider, he would have to kill him too or risk being reported, which would see him strung up over the matter as an abuse of authority. Instead, the guard figured it best just to carry out his orders and escort the oddly dressed young man to the city gates.

It was only a few short minutes before the group arrived at the city gates. This time there was no conversation between Wuffred and any of the guards. Instead, Wuffred gave a polite wave as he said thanks to his latest escort and continued walking down the road, away from the city.

After he felt he was far enough away to not be heard by the guards, Wuffred called out to Ammudien to make sure that he had made the journey too.

"Ammudien, please tell me that you are still behind me and that you have the shield," Wuffred requested in a loud whisper.

"Do not fret, my tall friend," Ammudien's voice said reassuringly. "Only I am not behind you but instead in front of you. And yes, I was able to procure Sagrim's Shield as expected."

"But," the invisible gnome continued, "we should not dally in such proximity to the city. I was unable to find a suitable decoy to place in the shield's case, so I suspect it won't be long now before someone notices our theft."

The news came as a surprise to Wuffred, who like Ammudien, had originally failed to consider that a shield for a gnome would be of a smaller size than a shield for the humans that occupied Tyleco. The berserker was quick to agree with his small friend, as the two hurried away from the city.

It was only when the pair had reached the edge of the city wall nearest the bandit camp where their friends waited that Ammudien finally dropped his invisibility and returned to the visible world for all to see. It was the first time that Wuffred was able to see the shield up close. He was sure of the shield's identity before, but now seeing the finely crafted shield and the familiar green shimmering metal that matched the material in the leggings Riorik had stashed away in his pack, Wuffred was more certain than ever that they had recovered the second piece of the Ascension Armor.

With the legendary shield in tow, the human and gnome quickly covered the last little distance back to their friends, who all rejoiced, including a much improved Riorik, at their return and the successful outcome of their mission.

Chapter 3

Asbin was not sure if it was just her nerves with Wuffred away again, if her secret pregnancy was having a greater effect than before, or if it was a combination of the two, but whatever it was, it had made the lone dwarf sicker than she had expected. The entire time Wuffred and Ammudien were away, she felt terribly sick to her stomach and vomited several times throughout the day. Before her sickness had been confined to the early morning hours, but today, it was much more significant and lasted for an extended period of time compared to before. The dwarf healer knew that she would not be able to hide her condition from the others for much longer.

She resolved to talk with Wuffred upon his return before announcing anything to the others though. Asbin felt it was only right to tell Wuffred first, since he was the father of her unborn child. But what she was going to tell him was something of a mystery that she had yet to answer.

Unfortunately, the day had passed faster than she had realized between her being sick and tending to Riorik's wound, which was all but a speck on the elf's back now. She had only just decided that she would talk with Wuffred about the life growing within her and started thinking of what she would say, when Wuffred and Ammudien's silhouettes could be seen approaching on the horizon.

The daring duo arrived at the camp just a few minutes later and was very eager to show the spoils of their adventure. Ammudien beamed with pride as he pulled the shield from its holster on his pack. A renewed Riorik and excited Nordahs clamored to get a closer look at their prize. Even Asbin had momentarily forgotten about her condition as she found herself in awe of the shield being passed around. For generations, her family had hunted these relics to no avail, and now she had held two of the four missing pieces in her hands.

The group squealed with glee and jumped around for the next few minutes. The excitement had made them all forget about the death that had followed them and surrounded them still. In fact, it was the growing stench of the rotting corpses outside the tower that pulled the group back to the reality of their situation and brought the celebration to an abrupt end.

"Ugh, no wonder you've been so sick Asbin. That smell is about to make me vomit too," Nordahs exclaimed, as his nose caught a whiff of a nearby body sitting in the day's heat.

Wuffred, with his adrenaline fading, also began to smell the rancid scent of death.

"Oh, my! That is indeed foul. Perhaps we should move on from this place and find someplace less smelly," the half-human berserker suggested to the party.

The others, having all smelled the unpleasant bouquet of fragrances, now stood with their noses covered as they desperately but ineffectively tried to block the foul smell. Everyone was quick to agree with Wuffred's suggestion, but this inexorably led to another question, one none there were prepared to answer.

"Okay, but where do we go from here?" Asbin asked in a very nasally voice, as she had resorted to pinching her nose closed with her fingers to spare herself from the nasty odor that now hung in the air like a fog over the entire area.

Nordahs and Wuffred only shrugged their shoulders in response to Asbin's question, as neither of them had any ideas to share. Riorik, having recovered as much mentally as he had physically, was quick to point to Ammudien but careful not open his mouth to avoid having to taste the rank air around them. Ammudien was forced to open his mouth to reply.

"Well, what do you expect me to do about it?" he asked in huff. "We are quite literally standing on top of a temple, so it isn't like I can detect magic from here. The temple's magic is too strong, and being so close to it, its magic would overshadow anything off in the distance that might tell me where our next objective lies."

He blinked his eyes several times, spat on the ground, and tried in vain to force the foul air from his nostrils after being forced to speak and breath more than he had wanted in the deteriorating environment.

Next, it was Riorik's turn to bite the bullet and open his mouth to the thick, disgusting smell that surrounded them all.

"We know there is nothing for us to the south. I vote we move north, away from here and try to get our bearings there, away from the temple and these bodies," Riorik stated, trying to be sure to sound convincing but without having to say more than was absolutely necessary.

It would not have mattered to the others how ludicrous Riorik's suggestion was, everyone was eager to be away from the growing stench, but everybody else was too distracted by the smell to think about anything else. In fact, little thought was actually given to Riorik's plan by anybody, but all of them quickly agreed to it.

The group made short work of packing up what items they had laying around the campsite and quickly headed off in a northerly direction to escape the smell of death that would forever be associated with what would be known as Dead Man's Hill to future generations, once the townsfolk of Tyleco discovered the full extent of carnage there.

Wuffred had told the group before about Wendy from the market and her family's farm just outside of town. Asbin was somewhat jealous of this mysterious Wendy woman who led Wuffred to her home, but she decided not to let her emotions get the better of her, at least not yet. The group moved towards the farmhouse, thinking that it would be a suitable distance from the tower to allow Ammudien to search for other signs of magic that might point them to the next relic.

Asbin and Wuffred walked at the back of the group. The dwarf knew this would probably be her best chance to talk with Wuffred about her state for a while.

"My love," she whispered up to the taller Wuffred, "I have something I need to tell you."

"What is it?" he calmly asked, without even looking down in Asbin's direction.

"Well," she started before taking a long, nervous pause, "it's something important that impacts us all but mostly you and I."

Her vague and cryptic statements were not making any sense to Wuffred. He finally turned to look at Asbin, as he cast a confused stare in her direction.

"Whatever do you mean?" he asked, completely oblivious to the facts and her subtle hints.

"I'm pregnant," she mouthed up at Wuffred.

Asbin was aware that Riorik and Nordahs could hear things at great distances, so she dared not to speak or even whisper the words out of fear that their conversation might be overheard. Alas, her efforts were for naught as the dense soon-to-be-father failed to catch on.

"What? Did you just say that you were pregnant?" he blurted out in his normal voice, completely missing the point behind Asbin's attempts at discretion.

This immediately got the attention of the others, who stopped in their tracks and turned to look at the couple.

"Asbin's pregnant?" asked Riorik.

"Wow, you two did not waste any time," exclaimed a shocked Nordahs.

Even Ammudien joined the conversation, but with less surprise and a more logic-based question.

"That does not make sense," he started.

"How can you be so sure? We have only been on this journey for a few weeks," the gnome added.

Asbin's cheeks turned a shade of bright red, in part from the embarrassment she now felt and in part from the anger she felt towards Wuffred for revealing her secret to the others so indiscriminately. She faced her friends and decided to confront the issue head-on.

"Yes, Wuffred and I are a couple. Yes, we have laid with one another. And, yes, I am pregnant. I can only attribute the sudden advancement in my pregnancy to the healing fountain. I had already started to suspect I was pregnant then, and I guess the fountain's magic accelerated my condition as it healed my injuries. I assume the fetus was in distress, thanks to my wounded condition, so the fountain encouraged its growth by healing it too," she stated as to answer that and any other questions the others may have.

She then turned back to Wuffred with a disappointed scowl on her whiskered face.

"I had hoped to discuss this with you first, in private, but it seems too late for that now."

Wuffred immediately realized his error but knew that there was nothing he could do about it now, other than apologize to Asbin.

"I'm sorry, my dear," he told her. "Your admission caught me by surprise, and I responded without thinking. I did not mean to share details of our relationship with the others without your consent."

Asbin could hear the sincerity in Wuffred's voice and see the shame in his eyes. She gave him a wink and a smile to show she believed him and understood. Then, she turned back to the group.

"But, we have a bigger problem," she said.

The others just stared at the dwarf, unsure of what other problem she spoke of.

"Any pregnancy is a delicate thing," she started. "Pregnancies can sap someone of their strength and stamina. Even now, we have all seen its effects on my ability to function with the constant sickness. As this pregnancy continues, I will be less and less capable of defending myself, and my friends, if another battle befalls us. And if I cannot defend myself, then that puts greater pressure on the group to try and pick up my slack. At some point, I will become a greater liability to you all than a benefit."

At first, nearly each of the male members of the group opened their mouths to refute Asbin's words, but they all thought better of it after a moment of reflection. They had all seen different pregnant people milling about in their hometowns. They remembered how they waddled about with their bulbous bellies, how they struggled to pick things up from the ground, the moans and groans about aching backs, and the look of pure exhaustion that many of them wore on their faces as they tried to keep up with their daily lives. There was no arguing with the dwarf that eventually she too would have these issues and that they would undoubtedly reduce her effectiveness as a fighter in their party.

"And let's not forget that we do not know how much longer our journey will last," Asbin continued, "and that there will come a time where I will have to deliver this baby. I do not get to pick and choose when that comes. It happens when it happens, regardless of what is going on around us. It is messy, it is painful, and it is loud. That is not something that would be very helpful, given the level of stealth that we have tried to maintain up to this point."

Again, the others wanted to counter Asbin's claims but knew them to be true, so they remained quiet. It was only after a short silence that Wuffred spoke up.

"So, what does all of this mean? What are you trying to say, my dearest Asbin?" he asked her.

She approached Wuffred, who promptly dropped to a kneeling position so that he could look into her face. With a single tear flowing down her cheek, the pregnant dwarf sweetly rubbed Wuffred's face. He could tell by the expression on her face what she was about to say.

"It means, it's time for me to say goodbye," she said softly. "I will not put you in jeopardy because I am unable to do my duty. I must return to Rhorm until our child is born."

Wuffred's reaction was immediate and firm.

"Then I will come with you," he demanded.

"No, sweet Wuffred, your place is here, with them," Asbin told him. "There is still much for Riorik to discover about his father's disappearance. You must continue with them as you promised. I will be in Rhorm waiting for you when your quest is complete, that you do not need to fear."

"But it is not safe for you to make such a long journey on your own, especially in such a condition. How will you get home?" a very concerned Wuffred asked.

"As we passed near the city wall earlier, I saw a dwarven trader pass through the gates. I presume he will return to Rhorm soon to resupply. I suspect I can barter for passage home on his wagon. Traders will do almost anything for coin, so surely a seat can be found for a paying customer. Besides, he would be shamed by the others back home if it were known that he refused to help a fellow dwarf."

"Are you sure that is wise, trusting a stranger like that?" questioned Ammudien.

"Given the circumstances, I'm not sure I have much other choice. I can remain alone here, I can ask the humans of Tyleco for help, I can attempt the trip to Rhorm on my own and on foot, or I can ask another dwarf for help. If it were you and you were faced with asking a strange human or a strange gnome for help, which would you pick?" she asked the mage.

"Point taken," was his reply.

It was common for races to trust strangers of their own race before trusting strangers of other races, so Ammudien could not find a fault in her logic, as he would ask a strange gnome for help before asking a strange human or dwarf. There was still a risk in asking any stranger for help, but it was much less likely that someone of your own race would mean you harm. In the earlier eras, when peace reigned, it would not have been as big of an issue. But, nowadays, with the races being so distrustful of one another, each race had become more dependent on their own kind so intraracial conflict was much less common than it was before.

"Should we see you off to Tyleco then?" Riorik inquired.

"What?" Nordahs yelled, obviously confused by his friend's quick acceptance of Asbin's plan.

"That's it? You're just going to send her home?" the young elf continued to ask his friend.

"Her mind is obviously made up, and besides, what she says is true. None of us can deny it. She needs to be somewhere safe, and that is not here with us. Her home is not even close to where we are, it is not safe for her to travel there alone, and a trader's wagon can get her home faster than we could by walking. I don't like the idea of her asking a stranger for help any more than you do, but I agree that it is probably the best chance she has at getting home."

The truth of Riorik's words stung inside his friend's pointed ears. Nordahs knew what Asbin had said to be the truth and knew that what Riorik said now was also true, but he did not want to accept it. He was given little other choice though. Asbin was clearly determined to leave before she became a bother to the others, and no amount of arguing would change that.

Riorik calmly placed a hand on his friend's shoulder and looked him in the eye.

"You know this is for the best. I want her here with us almost as badly as I'm sure Wuffred does, but her situation is much more complicated than ours now, and we must respect her wishes," Riorik told Nordahs, who nodded in agreement at his friend's sound logic and calming voice.

Being ever-mindful of his companions and their feelings, Riorik approached Wuffred and Asbin as Wuffred stood to greet him.

"Wuffred," Riorik said, "we will gladly wait here if you would like to escort Asbin near the city gates and say your farewells."

The young elf knew that this moment had to be harder on his half-human friend than the rest of them, so he wanted to be sure that he gave Wuffred ample opportunity, and some privacy, to send away the person that the berserker obviously cared the most about. It was a sign of great respect and friendship that Wuffred did not miss. Riorik's gesture was almost as touching to Wuffred as the thought of he and Asbin having a child together. Both thoughts nearly made the tough berserker cry.

"Thank you, Riorik," was all Wuffred could manage to say, as he tried to express his gratitude for his friend's understanding and kindness.

The two friends shook hands before Riorik turned his attention to the short mother-to-be.

"And Asbin, I hope that you find safe travels home, where you will rest and look after the life blossoming inside your womb. Once our quest is complete, we will come to Rhorm to meet your new child and reunite your family."

His words choked up the dwarf, who could not manage a response out of fear that she would break down in tears if she tried. Instead, she nodded her head vigorously before embracing the young elf. She did not want to admit it, but she was fearful that this might be the last time she saw them. Their quest was a dangerous one and they had already experienced a lot of trauma, so she knew that it was likely they would face even more in the days ahead.

Nordahs and Ammudien understood that this was to be their chance to say their farewells to the dwarf before her imminent departure. The elf and gnome walked over to where Asbin stood with the others. They each took turns hugging the dwarf and offering their well-wishes and goodbyes.

Asbin took the pouch that held what remained of her concoction used to treat Riorik's poisonous wound and handed it to Riorik.

"Take this, just in case the wound is not fully healed," she told the Elven Ranger, who gladly accepted the ointment.

"We'll wait for you here. Take all of the time you need," Riorik reminded Wuffred, as the berserker and healer walked away from the group and towards the city.

***

After several minutes of walking, Asbin and Wuffred approached the gated wall that surrounded the city of Tyleco. This was Wuffred's third visit to the gate in the past two days, so he was hesitant to get too close. As they got closer, his pace slowed but he was reticent about why. Asbin just figured that he was tired, after all, he had made the journey to the city and back several times recently.

"So, what's your plan?" Wuffred asked his beloved.

"Well, I figured that I would just wait out here for the dwarf merchant to leave and then try to bargain with him for a lift home," she answered.

Wuffred was surprised by the simplicity of her plan and partly shocked that it included her just loitering around the gates of a human town, hoping to catch a dwarven trader passing by.

"Why don't you go find the trader in the town's market and barter with him there?" he asked.

"Honestly? I'm somewhat afraid to enter a human town," she answered. "Plus, I don't even know what I would tell the guards to get them to let me pass."

Wuffred had not thought of that. He also struggled to come up with a plan to gain her entrance past the guards. At first, he thought of telling the guards that she was the merchant's wife that followed him to the city, but that story seemed illogical the more he thought about it. The merchant arrived on a horse-drawn wagon, and she arrived on foot. How would she be able to explain how she was able to follow behind so closely on foot? What if her lie was discovered by the guards, perhaps by the merchant himself? There were several risks and issues with that plan, but Wuffred failed to come up with anything better.

But, luck was with the dwarf this day. As the pair talked about her plan and the various other ideas that ultimately were rejected for being too risky or silly, the gates opened and a cart rolled out behind a raggedy looking horse. The cart was being driven by a dwarf. Was it the same dwarf merchant she had seen enter from a distance before? She had no way of knowing, but she was not going to let that stop her now.

"Excuse me," she called out to the other dwarf, as the cart approached her location.

The driver slowed the cart to a stop just in front of Asbin. The male dwarf seated at the front of the wagon gave a hard look at Wuffred, who was standing too close to Asbin for his comfort.

"Are you under duress from this human?" the stranger asked, as he continued to glare in Wuffred's direction.

"Heavens no," Asbin quickly replied.

"This young man has offered me kindness in helping me reach the city," she explained, not wanting to reveal the true nature of their relationship.

"I see. And what is it that you require of me?" the still suspicious dwarven driver asked.

Asbin quickly came up with a new lie.

"I traveled with my father, who was a merchant like yourself, but we recently fell victim to highwaymen. My father tried to fight them, but they outnumbered and overpowered him. He held them off long enough that I could run away, but the brutes killed him and took our buggy full of merchandise. I only seek the means to return to Rhorm so that I may see to his spirit and rebuild his business."

The merchant knew that highwaymen were a constant threat on the roads between cities for people like himself, so her story seemed plausible. Even still, he was somewhat leery of the strange dwarf who carried a shield and mace—not the typical tools of a merchant or a merchant's daughter. But, it only took one sentence to persuade him to overlook that mistrust and her questionable outfit.

"I have coin and can pay you for a ride," Asbin offered.

The dwarf's greed kicked in, and his concerns were instantly overshadowed by his desire for money.

"You'll pay up front," he demanded, "or else I will leave you here."

The two went back and forth for the next couple of minutes, as they bargained with one another before settling on a final price for Asbin's ride home. The merchant explained that his route was not a direct one but first saw him visiting Kern and Dresdin. Asbin used this to barter for a cheaper price in exchange for her help at those stops. She had hoped for a direct trip to Rhorm, but the other dwarf demanded too high of a price to skip those stops, so it was either that or wait for another dwarf and hope for better. In the end, Asbin decided this was her best chance and the two stops would only be a slight delay in her return and still faster than if she tried to make the trip on foot.

The two eventually reached an agreement, so Asbin pulled out her share of the coins from the bandit loot they had recovered and counted out the payment amount. The greedy dwarf quickly grabbed the collection of small metallic coins from Asbin's hand and shoved them into the coin purse hanging on his belt.

With the sum paid, Asbin climbed into the back of the cart and said a goodbye to Wuffred, while being careful not to reveal their relationship to her fellow dwarf. She watched Wuffred fade away, as the cart thundered off towards the merchant's next stop.

Wuffred waited for the cart to disappear over the horizon before he started his return to his friends. It was hard for him to watch Asbin ride off without him, but her words echoed in his mind of how his place was here and how his friends needed him. He had made a promise to Riorik and Nordahs, and it was his duty to see that promise fulfilled, no matter what his heart desired.

With a heart full of sadness, Wuffred began the lonely walk back to the others. His thoughts were of Asbin with every step, which seemed to make his feet heavy and slow, but he forced himself to carry on.

***

Meanwhile, while Riorik and the others waited for Wuffred's return, the trio discussed their next step. They now had in their possession two pieces of the Ascension Armor, had developed a theory of what caused Riorik's father's madness, but still lacked proof of that cause or proof of what happened after his disappearance.

"I think we need to keep searching for the other missing pieces," Riorik suggested.

"To what end?" Nordahs asked his friend.

Nordahs was beginning to question the value of continuing their search. Having searched two tombs—one being the same tomb Cyrel fell into at the same time he was said to have gone mad—they had not found any clues to Cyrel's whereabouts. Sure, they had confirmed the existence of the Ascension Armor and carried two of the legendary items with them, but the young elf was unable to reconcile within his mind how those items held the answer to what happened to Riorik's father years earlier. Instead, Nordahs was becoming more concerned with how he could return to Rishdel without being branded a traitor and tossed into the stockades.

Before Riorik had a chance to answer, Ammudien spoke up.

"Because we are not alone in our search, that is why," the gnome said.

"These gnolls and orcs," Ammudien continued, "are not acting on their own. Someone controls them from afar, and if their brutality is any indication of the ruthlessness of their master, then we cannot allow such powerful items to fall into their hands. Think about the bloodshed and violence that has already reached these lands, just in pursuit of these items. Now, think about how much more bloodshed and violence would be released upon us all if this malevolent force acquired these items with their legendary powers. Imagine the threat something like that would pose to your home and to your family."

"Forget my mission, forget Riorik's quest," the mage continued in his speech. "There is a growing threat out there that is bigger than any one of us, a threat that the people hiding behind their walls and fences from one another are likely ignorant to, and it is up to us to do our part in preventing a larger tragedy to befall Corsallis. I will not see in my lifetime another devastation across these lands like the one my ancestors saw when they battled the Black Dragon, a foul beast summoned through the now banned dark arts."

The small gnome spoke with much conviction and emotion. It was something that he clearly felt very strongly about. Nordahs correctly assumed that Ammudien was somehow connected to the terrible tragedy the gnome now referenced from a past era. Ammudien came from a long line of mages, some very powerful mages at the time of the Black Dragon's rise. Those ancestors were called up to help fight the destructive demonic dragon, and all died. The dragon was extremely powerful, and they posed little resistance before the beast's true weakness was found. In the wake of their defeat, Ammudien's ancestors and the other mages who similarly failed were considered martyrs among the gnomes and mages, but it also created higher expectations of their descendants, a burden that Ammudien still carried with him.

"O…kay," Nordahs said, unsure of how else to respond to the gnome's impassioned speech.

Riorik took the speechlessness of his friend as an opportunity to contribute to the conversation that he had been locked out of, thanks to Ammudien's passionate words.

"Ammudien is right," Riorik started. "I stand firm in my belief that this armor holds the key to my father's disappearance, but knowing that someone else is looking for them and doing so by using such ferocious forces as gnolls and orcs means we must not let them succeed. It's actually a win-win for us to do so, when you think about it."

Ammudien shot Riorik a confused look at that last statement.

"Think about it," Riorik replied to the gnome's puzzled expression. "If we find the remaining pieces, then we all stand a better chance at seeing our personal goals completed. But at the same time, in doing so, we stop whatever evil force that seeks what we already have. We get the answers we seek and become heroes in the process."

His exuberance was a bit of sham though. He remembered the close calls they had already faced to get this far, and now, with Asbin's departure, he knew the road ahead would most likely be more difficult. But, he held onto his façade because he did not want to worry his friends.

Nordahs was outnumbered. Ammudien and Riorik clearly wanted to forge ahead, and they both made compelling arguments as to why. The elf relented to his friends and their desires.

"So, how do we continue from here?" he asked, making his capitulation clear.

"Now that we are no longer standing directly on top of the last temple," Ammudien began, "I should be able to use my detection spell to see if I can sense the presence of another tomb. That would give us our next destination."

"That sounds easy enough," Nordahs said agreeably. "That approach has proven useful and accurate before, so I see no reason to change now."

As he had several times before, Ammudien moved a few feet away from the others and went through the familiar motions to cast the spell that the group had become accustomed to seeing.

He faced due north, as he began sweeping his hands first to the west and then to the east. When he moved his hands westward, his spell showed no signs of reaction to any significant magical presence. However, the more he moved to the east, the more his hands began to light up. When he faced in a northeasterly direction, just north of Kern, the spell gave the familiar reaction that was seen when the mage's spell detected the most recent temple. Ammudien wasted no time in extinguishing the fire-like glow that enveloped his hands before returning to his friends.

"So, to the northeast?" Riorik asked as Ammudien approached his location.

"It would seem so, yes," the grinning gnome replied.

With the direction decided, the group waited for Wuffred's return. Once he had rejoined his friends, they filled him in on the findings from Ammudien's spell. Wuffred, eager to complete this journey so that he might return to Asbin, urged the group to depart immediately.

"Well, the sooner we get started then the sooner we can arrive there," he told the others.

The human turned and started walking in the direction the others told him the next temple would be found. His friends hurried to catch up to the forlorn berserker. The group was now unknowingly headed towards the oasis of Narsdin and on a collision course with the masked leader of Macadre, who rode

towards the oasis to meet his mysterious agent known only as K.

Chapter 4

As day turned to night, the veiled rider continued to spur his horse forward. He was nearing the towering mountain range that separated Macadre from the other cities. It was a massive natural defense that allowed him to grow his kingdom in private and could also provide a great defense from invaders with its high peaks and few narrow passageways. But now, those same features slowed his advance south.

The mountains were notorious for bad weather, and as he drew closer to their location, the sky darkened and a slow rain began to fall. It was an ominous sign. The slow rain now meant that heavier rains were coming, which would make the rocky slopes and narrow trails sloppy and slippery. This also meant that some passages through the mountains would not be safe to traverse in such inclement conditions.

When Grue and his troops passed this way just weeks earlier, they had used a little-known land bridge that crossed a gully in the eastern end of the mountain range. Typically, that route would be the fastest, despite it being farther away from the oasis than other pathways. But, in this weather, that path was almost certain death, especially on horseback. The determined king was now forced to take a slower path, which would be even slower now thanks to the poor weather. It was frustrating to the anxious rider, but there was no other choice.

Eager to get as far through the mountains as possible before the trails became washed out and impassable, the rider dug his heels into the poor beast that carried him along. The saddled horse tossed his head about, shaking some of the water from its mane before galloping ahead at its top speed. The armored rider held tight to the reigns but even tighter to the horse with his knees and legs. Rider and horse raced across the land and forward into the coming storm.

After several minutes of fast-paced riding and mud being slung from the horse's hooves, the pair arrived at the base of the mountains. The rain had changed from a slow fall to a steady stream of water. The crashing thunder and constant flashes of lightning signaled that a downpour was still in store for them.

Macadre's leader pulled back hard on the reigns to bring his mount to a halt. Between the increasing darkness and rain, he had misjudged the entry point to the path into the mountains that he'd wanted to take. The masked individual took a moment to scan the area and regain his bearings. It did not take long for the sharp-eyed rider to realize that he was several yards west of where he wanted to be. He tugged on the reigns and led the horse in the proper direction.

The rain had been falling here for some time it seemed, as it was immediately obvious that the ground was completely saturated. The mud and clay squished with each of the horse's steps, and its hooves were already beginning to sink into the soft ground. This caused the horse's progress to be slow, very slow, despite its rider's constant urging to move faster.

As he repeatedly kicked his horse in an unsuccessful attempt to motivate the skittish animal to sprint through the muddy mountainside, the self-appointed king could not help but think about what impact such weather may have on his troops, who should be following close behind. Large formations usually do not move with great speed to begin with, so if confronted with terrain like this, it was likely that the group could be delayed for a long time. He was anxious to put his invasion plan into action, but that plan would only work after all of his troops had crossed the mountain pass. The thought of his plan being interrupted only added to his frustration, causing him to kick his horse even harder.

The progress got even slower as they made their way higher and higher through the mountains. Eventually, the rain did begin to stop, but it had managed to wash out several parts of the trail and make other parts impossible to move through quickly. There were even a few rock slides, which blocked the path and required the impatient king to get down from his saddle and manually clear the path before moving on.

The sky grew darker and darker as the night passed, but the leader with the covered face refused to rest until daylight. K's message was clear—another piece of the armor awaited him at the oasis. There was an intense desire to possess the powerful item as soon as it was possible, especially if his agent's earlier report was correct and someone else was seeking the same thing. He felt certain that the other person looking for the missing armor was Whilem and knowing that Whilem had fled Nectana told him that if he did not recover the piece now, then it was probably just a matter of time before Whilem did. He had no idea that Whilem was already dead and not the competition the mysterious K had alluded to, but either way, he was not willing to take the chance that Whilem or anybody else might get their hands on whatever piece rested at the oasis before he could.

As he pushed through the night, there were times that he was forced to dismount and lead the stubborn equine down steep, slippery trails or across rocky ledges that it did not want to traverse willingly. There was more than one occasion when the armed rider contemplated just killing the horse and being free of the beast's opposition, but he always thought better of it because he knew that after the mountains, the horse's speed would serve him better than his own.

As difficult as it was, Macadre's leader pressed on in pursuit of his goal. He knew it was unlikely that he would reach the other side of the mountain pass tonight, but he was determined to get as close as possible. He figured he could rest at the oasis after he acquired the armor, while waiting for his troops to arrive as planned.

***

Knowing that their leader had left the palace headed for the oasis, the generals and commanders of the troops hurried to complete their preparations. None of them knew the real reason behind his sudden departure but assumed that their immediate presence was required. The messenger had only told a few people about their leader's decree that tomorrow was the latest they could leave for the oasis meeting point, and those people were not the people in charge. The messenger had told some of the lieutenants about the updated order and assumed they would let their commanding officers know, but they expected the messenger to pass the word along.

"I don't care if you haven't slept yet," one general shouted at a soldier who had complained to another soldier, but not quietly enough, about the prospect of marching throughout the night.

Soldiers scurried through the barracks near the docks as they hurried to fill their rucksacks with provisions. Others ran from smith to smith to find which smith they had given their armor to for repairs upon their return. But, even more scrambled to find a blacksmith who could sharpen their blades that had chipped in fights or even dulled over time.

Every forge in Macadre burned hot as the blacksmiths and their apprentices struggled to keep up with the demand. The smiths had already been working around the clock to produce new equipment and goods for the swelling ranks of the army as gnolls, orc, trolls, humans, elves, and pretty much any able-bodied figure in the region were conscripted for the coming war. That demand now combined with the sudden influx of repairs was too much for the artisans to keep up with. This infuriated the generals, who now felt even more rushed than before to start marching after their commander-in-chief.

There were even some of the generals who instructed those under their command to leave whatever items they lacked behind.

"If you don't have a weapon now, there will be plenty to pick from later on the battlefield," one general could be heard shouting to one of his platoons.

"Armor is a luxury, not a requirement," another could be heard yelling at a troll desperately looking for a helmet.

It was chaos in the streets and shops of Macadre. There was no chance that the troops would be fully outfitted if they marched immediately. Even waiting until the next day, it would still be difficult to pull off, but those left in charge wrongly assumed that they needed to be on the move now. It was apparent that the troops would be under-equipped regardless, but nobody dared to contradict their master.

It was not much longer before the calls to form up and prepare to march rang out.

"Fall in!" was the shout that could be heard coming from various ranking soldiers.

The chaos that had ruled before was quickly replaced with order, as the veteran soldiers moved into position and helped the newer 'recruits' follow suit. The army's numbers had swelled considerably, and the different formations of infantry, archers, warg riders, orcs, and trolls filled the many cobblestone streets. Even many of the residents of Nectana had been ushered to the region's capital in preparation for this moment.

The order that came over the city as the troops fell into rank and file was short-lived though. With the groups spread out down several streets and alleys, when it was time for everyone to move, there was no coordination or planning. Everyone started moving at the same time. At every intersection, it seemed that different groups were colliding. This naturally sparked several fights and arguments that only served to slow their departure. There were no serious injuries, but it certainly highlighted the lack of cohesion, especially among the newer members of the army.

The commanders struggled to regain control of their troops, but eventually, order was restored. Once the lines were formed again, the different leaders realized that it was best for them to come up with a marching order to avoid similar issues and outbursts again.

After much talking and chest puffing, it was agreed that rank and seniority would determine the order that each leader and their group would march in, with the most senior officers taking the lead and the lower ranking officers bringing up the rear. It was not the ideal plan for those relegated to the back of the marching order, but ultimately, it was an order from a superior, so they were left with little choice but to follow it.

The group's second attempt to march out of town went much smoother, allowing the hundreds of soldiers that made up Macadre's army to exit through the city's iron barred gates and across the thick wooden drawbridge that spanned the trap-laden moat surrounding the city's simple stone walls. The procession of troops could be seen for hundreds of feet. It took several minutes for the full force to pass through the city's only entrance before they headed off towards the rain-soaked mountains.

***

Captain Cooper, having witnessed Wuffred and Asbin's parting from the parapet that lined the top of the Tyleco's city wall, had remained in the shadows as he followed Wuffred back to the others. He had remained suspicious of Wuffred's story and seeing the young human in the company of a dwarf, he was now sure of Wuffred's deceit. Wuffred said he had a sister who was wounded, but Asbin was anything but his sister and showed no signs of an injury. He was intent on finding out the truth about Wuffred and bringing him to justice in Tyleco if necessary.

The guard captain watched in pure astonishment to see that Wuffred was traveling with two elves and a gnome. Tyleco saw a variety of traders from other cities, enabling him to recognize Ammudien as a gnome, even though gnomes were the city's rarest non-human visitors. But, it was the presence of the two elves, Riorik and Nordahs, that shocked the veteran guard the most.

The wood elves of Rishdel were very reclusive and never emerged from the woods. The water elves of Aqtarios had not been seen or heard from in decades, leaving most in the region to believe that they had died or emigrated to some foreign land. And, the dark elves were so hated that they never ventured outside of the Narsdin region.

Seeing Wuffred not only in the company of two elves but obviously on friendly terms, and dressed similarly, left Captain Cooper scratching his head in confusion.

"I knew that boy was lying, but this is unbelievable," he thought to himself as he watched the four friends interact when Wuffred returned.

Captain Cooper then took a moment to rationalize what he was seeing and determine his next move. His thoughts revealed his paranoia but also his dedication.

"Perhaps he is acting as a spy or a rogue. The group he travels with could easily infiltrate and interact with citizens in every town of Corsallis, each acting as a scout for the cities of their race."

"Could this boy and his companions be more of Draynard's thieves, here to steal Lord Veyron's birthright in another bid to claim the throne for his own? Perhaps they are mercenaries hired by one of Lord Veyron's cousins, sent here to assassinate our beloved lord so they can usurp his crown."

"The only way to truly uncover this treachery is to follow this liar and discover the truth once and for all. I must do my duty to route villainy and conspiracy at all costs, to protect this city, my family, and above all, Lord Veyron."

The captain had to remain a fair distance away to avoid detection, which meant he could not hear what the group discussed, but it was obvious that there was some excitement among them. Judging by the actions of the others and the constant pointing towards the northeast, Captain Cooper felt comfortable that there was something of interest to the group in that direction. He knew nothing about what lay northeast or what such an odd group of travelers might find interesting there, but he knew he was going to follow them and find out.

As he looked around from his hiding spot behind a large tree, he noticed the daylight was beginning to fade. The growing darkness made him assume that the group would most likely make camp for the night and head out in the morning. He was wrong. Captain Cooper was busy looking for where he might bed down for the night too, so he was quite surprised when he looked up to see the group walking off in the direction they had pointed earlier.

Concerned they may be headed to a larger group or campsite, Captain Cooper stayed in his position behind the tree until the group was almost over the horizon and beyond his sight. This left with him little choice but to move from the tree's safety and concealment if he was to keep the strangers within sight. Luckily for the experienced soldier and guard, the grass around the farmland had several large patches used for growing various grains that had tall stalks, which he was able to use to remain hidden from view.

The tall grains did have a drawback though. While they provided ample cover for the stalking city guard, they also obscured his view of his target, making it difficult for him to accurately track them without occasionally standing up to gain his bearings. This put him at great risk of being seen by Wuffred and the others, but it was still safer than moving about in the open under the night's natural light. With no other stealthy options available, Captain Cooper continued his pursuit.

The group seemed to be moving with purpose, without concern for bandits or beasts that knowingly use the cover of night to stalk their prey. Captain Cooper found it difficult to keep up with the group while he remained hidden from view, especially once they moved beyond the cover of the farmland fields.

Once past the tall stalks of the farmer's grains, Captain Cooper was forced to move through the open terrain while squatting down to minimize his shadow. The constant crouching and bending made it tough for the older human. The muscles in his legs began to ache, as did his joints and back. The proud city guard captain refused to give up the chase, despite the aches and pains that were steadily growing throughout his body.

But, the experienced warrior was not fool enough to think that he could continue forever. Captain Cooper knew that he would eventually have to stop and rest his weary frame. This meant that he could very likely lose track of Wuffred and his friends. To lose sight of them would mean the end of his pursuit. This left Captain Cooper with a decision to make: to follow as far as he could before resting and hoping that he did not lose the trail or to abandon his chase now and return to Tyleco so that he could rest in his own bed tonight.

It was then that Captain Cooper's luck looked to have changed for the better.

Just as the captain had reached the decision to call off his chase and return to his wife and home in Tyleco, the dedicated guard noticed that his targets had stopped a short distance ahead and appeared to be setting up camp for the night. This spurred the leader of Tyleco's city guard to remain vigilant in his pursuit of the suspected criminal and obvious liar, Wuffred. Captain Cooper was relieved at the thought that he could rest his weary body without too much risk of losing his target before the morning's light shone over the horizon's edge.

Captain Cooper had made the decision to follow Wuffred rather suddenly, so he was ill-prepared to camp a night in the wilderness. With no provisions or even a simple bedroll, this would not be the comfortable night in his bed snuggled next to his wife that he had imagined earlier in the day. With little other options available to him, Captain Cooper set about finding the most comfortable spot on the ground that he could. In the end, the ground is the ground and no real comfort could be found on its hard, uneven surface. He did manage to pile up a fair amount of soft, green grass to cobble together the makings of a basic pillow-like headrest on which he could lay his head for the night.

With his pitiful excuse for a bed made, Captain Cooper laid down in hopes of getting at least some rest for the unknown journey that lay ahead.

Chapter 5

"Hey, Ammudien, do you think we should check the area to make sure it's safe before we finish setting up camp?" a nervous Nordahs asked his gnome friend.

"Do we really think it necessary?" the tired gnome replied.

Ammudien's little legs had been working hard to keep up with Wuffred's motivated pace, so the thought of doing anything else before curling up to get some rest was not high on the gnome's list of priorities.

Unsure of how to respond, Nordahs just scratched his head at Ammudien's question. But, before the dumbfounded Ranger could respond, the voice of his friend saved him.

"Of course, we do the check," Riorik said casually.

"Who knows what foul animals roam these parts. Besides, we still don't know who else may be searching for these relics or where they may be," the young elf continued.

Ammudien hung his head at Riorik's words. Casting the spell did not cause him any distress, but the small gnome was exhausted and wanted nothing more than to sleep. Riorik's response just meant that sleep would have to wait for a few more minutes is all.

"The way that Whilem character lunged for the leggings in your backpack, don't you think he was the other person looking for the pieces?" Wuffred asked, convinced that the barbarian was the one they had been racing unknowingly all this time.

"I must admit that it seemed odd, how he grabbed for them like he knew what he was looking for, but a barbarian seems like an odd person to have gnolls and orcs running about doing his dirty work, especially since he was right there too. And there was an air of sincerity to him when he spoke about the death of his sister and how he lusted for revenge. If he sought revenge against orcs for her death, then he is unlikely to have been their leader," Riorik rationalized as part of his response to Wuffred.

Wuffred could find no fault in Riorik's logic, so he gave a slight shrug of his shoulders and a nod of his head in acceptance of the elf's theory.

Riorik, now finished with Wuffred, turned his attention back to the gnome that started the whole conversation.

"Ammudien, please, just do a quick check. Your magic is superior to even my keen eyes for such a search, and now that we are without a healer, I would feel much better knowing that we won't get mauled in our sleep," he politely requested of his mage friend.

The elf's words hit home for the mage, who had forgotten about Asbin's absence in his tired state. If there was an attack on the group during the night, with himself being the smallest one, Ammudien was the most likely target for an ambushing predator like a cougar or puma. And, without a healer among them now, if he were injured, it would be a greater problem for him so far from home or a friendly town.

Ammudien, having come to terms with the apparent delay to his sleep, stepped away from the group, which was his normal nature when doing his magical checks. The gnome knelt to the ground, the same as before, and began muttering silently the mystical words required to evoke the spell that would secure his rest. His hands erupted in the familiar flame effect to signal the spell was being performed. Ammudien concentrated on the ripples he felt in the lands around their campsite.

The spell's ripples, at first, detected what the gnome already knew. Aside from his constant presence, the gnomish mage could feel the footsteps of Riorik, Nordahs, and Wuffred as they moved about setting up their campsite. As he felt the ripples expand beyond, he was able to sense some small animals—squirrels, rats, some small dogs or cats, maybe. He was not able to really make out what type of animals he detected, but he could tell that they were small and of little threat or concern to him and his friends. However, what Ammudien detected next was surprising.

A fair distance behind the group, the mage's magic detected the presence of something large. Ammudien tried to focus on the unknown object's ripples but was unable to make out any details. Whatever it was that his magic had revealed seemed to be stationary, making it impossible for the small spell caster to make out how many feet it walked on or any clue really that might tell him what manner of life this was. All that the ripples could show him was that the mysterious presence was big, weighed over two-hundred pounds, and seemed as if it was laying on the ground, perhaps asleep. The main thing that really concerned Ammudien about this was that it laid directly in the path that the group had walked not long before, and they found no signs of anything being there or having been there recently, so whatever this was had just arrived.

"Could this thing be following us?" he wondered to himself, as he continued unsuccessfully trying to make out the unknown lifeform's true identity.

"Should I warn the others?" he also pondered briefly before deciding it best to err on the side of caution rather than risk his or his friends' safety in the night's darkness.

Confident that the unknown presence was still stationary and what his next steps would be, Ammudien continued to check the area with his spell. He turned his attention to any ripples in the other directions but continued to find nothing else significant or that he considered threatening. The gnome completed his spell, extinguished the artificial flames that had enveloped his hands, and calmly returned to the area designated for the night's camp.

"And?" Riorik asked as Ammudien approached.

"Well, I have some good news and some *other* news," Ammudien replied, still perplexed by the unknown presence behind their campsite.

The others did not know what to make of the mage's unusual answer, so nobody spoke up right away. The three non-magical friends each exchanged looks with questioning expressions, hoping that someone else might understand what Ammudien was alluding to with his comment.

Finally, Wuffred decided to find out.

"What do you mean 'good news and some *other* news'?" he asked.

"Well," Ammudien began, "the good news is that I didn't detect any obvious threats or the presence of a large force amassed nearby."

"And the '*other* news'?" Wuffred asked hesitantly.

"There was something else out there, but I was unable to determine what it was or if its presence poses any threat to us," the mage sheepishly answered, obviously somewhat embarrassed that he failed to understand more about the unexplained ripple.

"Whatever it is, it seemed to be lying still on the ground, exactly along the path we walked. But, it is big. It reminded me of ripples like Wuffred when he sleeps," Ammudien added, obviously still trying to solve the riddle of what the ripple could be.

"So, it's a person?" Nordahs asked.

"Do you think someone is following us? Like maybe a bandit who may have fled the battle or another gnoll?" Nordahs added.

"It's hard to say," Ammudien answered. "The spell can only detect the presence of other beings, as I've said before, so I can only speculate to the presence's true nature. And, to make matters worse, the fact that it is sitting still makes it more difficult to distinguish any characteristics that might help to distinguish it as man or beast, so we are left with only our assumptions and fears to guide the way."

"Do you think it is worth investigating?" asked a still calm Riorik.

Ammudien looked at his friend, unsure of how to answer.

"Just tell me, Ammudien, do you think it poses enough of a threat to have us backtrack to its location to determine if it poses a threat or not? If you are unsure, then we can always set up a rotating watch like we have in the past so that others can rest while someone keeps an open eye out for any signs of danger."

"I think if we just do a watch, that should suffice," Ammudien answered.

The gnome was too tired to walk back for what might just be an animal that happened across their path. Riorik's suggestion of a watch rotation was not ideal because it meant the gnome's sleep would be interrupted, but it was something that he had grown accustomed to with this group.

There was some discussion among the group about how long each rotation would last, who would be watching in what order, and most importantly, who went first. Ultimately, Ammudien successfully argued that his earlier work detecting the unknown entity counted as his turn, allowing him to sleep now and take the final watch later. Wuffred and Nordahs whined until Riorik agreed that he would take the first watch. The remaining two were still unable to agree on the order for their turns, so Riorik took the responsibility to dictate that Wuffred would go after him and Nordahs would go after Wuffred. The berserker was not overjoyed with Riorik's decision but opted not to argue with his friend, especially since it was he who urged them to rush forward so late in the day.

***

As the morning's light grew brighter and brighter, the leader and his horse continued to make their way through the treacherous mountain pass. The rains had stopped during the night, but the flowing waters that rushed down the mountainsides had done their damage. Even after the rain had stopped, the pair's movement had continued at a slowed pace, thanks to the muddy conditions and slippery ground beneath their feet and hooves. Nevertheless, he had persevered throughout the night and now found himself nearing the path's exit to the valley below.

It was a short ride, short but sketchy, and was anything but quick or problem free. There was more than one instance of the tired horse's hooves slipping and sliding in the mud. There was even a time where the rain-soaked ground collapsed under the weight of the beast and its rider, causing the horse to rear up on its hind legs to avoid falling within the muddy soil. This act threw the horse's lone occupant from his saddle and onto the ground with a painful thud. The heavily armored rider figured it would be easier to lead his mount the rest of the way down the path, since the horse was too slow and cautious for his liking at this point.

He grabbed his trained, but apparently not too well trained, horse by the bridle and led the four-legged animal down the trail. Rider and horse walked side by side along the soupy pathway. The horse's owner spent the entire walk chastising the horse for its perceived poor performance, trying to traverse the tricky environment under inclement weather conditions. Anything less than perfection was unacceptable to the overly anxious rider.

On foot, the path was much longer than expected, but the two did eventually find its end. This meant it was now time for the second part of their journey to the oasis, but this would be the longest part. The mountains were closer to Macadre than the oasis, but due to the hazardous features of the mountain, it was just slow to cross. Now, in the open, dry, empty desert plains of southern Narsdin, it was a very long ride. All the eager rider could do was hope that the weather would not cause similar delays along this section of his route. If the land was dry, the horse could carry its passenger to his destination by the day's end, but there was no way to know the condition of the ground ahead without pressing on.

Once more, Macadre's leader hauled his armored frame back into the thin leather saddle strapped to the horse. After getting seated on the horse's back again, he wasted no time in trying to spur his horse into a full gallop. The horse was tired after the night's trek, so there was some resistance. The horse whinnied, neighed, and even bucked slightly at his repeated attempts to force the animal into a full sprint.

This annoyed the horse's rider immensely, but he was not willing to give up so easily to the arguments of a simple animal. He extended his urges to using the extra leather from the reigns as a whip so that now he was whipping the horse with the reigns and essentially kicking the horse with the heels of his armored feet. Eventually, the horse relented and moved from a simple trot to a high-speed gallop.

The ground beyond the mountains was in much better condition. The sandy nature of the desert plains absorbed most of the water that fell there, but generally there was far less rain in that area compared to the mountains with their high, snow-covered peaks. This allowed the horse to move much faster than it had during the night but still not as fast as the rider would have liked. The shifting sands meant that the horse was unable to maintain a full gallop. This allowed the exhausted horse some time to rest and try to cool down, but the individual on the horse's back was not interested in what the horse wanted, only what he wanted.

The two reached the oasis later in the day, the light had already begun to fade. It had taken longer than expected to reach the oasis, but his fast-paced approach had gotten him there much sooner than if he had waited to march with his troops.

As the rider approached the small pool of water surrounded by a few small, simple trees, he could see his agent, the mysterious K, waiting by its edge. The horse's hooves on the soft sand made little noise, but the rider's armor clanged as the horse made its way closer to the oasis. K, alerted by the armor's noise, stood to greet his benefactor.

K was nearly as tall as Narsdin's king when the two stood side by side. His loyal agent also seemed intent on keeping his face and other physical attributes hidden. K was dressed in a long-sleeved robe that covered his entire body, down to the very tips of his fingers. The robe was complete with a large hood that covered the agent's head and cast a dark shadow over his face, making it impossible for anyone to see unless they got very close.

The only part of K's identity that could be discerned was his sex. K spoke with a deep baritone voice, a sound that was something extremely rare for most females in Corsallis regardless of race, so it was a reasonable assumption for those that heard him speak to correctly assume his gender as male.

Probably the most unusual thing about K was how he interacted with the covered king from the North. Where most who addressed him kneeled and were careful to avoid any direct eye contact, K seemed content to look upon the shrouded figure and even embrace him with a hearty handshake. The relationship between the two was very different from the relationship of fear and subjugation that the leader had with the people of Macadre.

"I'm pleased to see you," K said as he greeted the weary rider.

"You look tired. It was surely a long ride. Would you like to get some rest?" he asked the masked leader.

K's guest had no intention to rest just yet.

"No," he answered from behind his mask. "Your message said you knew where another piece of the armor was and that it was here. I will obtain the armor before resting. My troops march this way as we speak, and I desire to be ready at their arrival."

"Very well," K replied.

K turned and pointed to the waters of the oasis. The tip of a slender finger could barely be seen extending beyond the cuff of the robe's sleeve.

"Your armor lies there," the king's agent said casually.

"Am I to believe that at the bottom of this shallow pool lies another piece of the Ascension Armor? Explain yourself, K," the confused leader demanded.

"Yes," K began in his deep voice, "the next piece lies beneath the water. However, this 'shallow pool', as you put it, is more than it appears. The pool was created using magic. It sits above the armor's hiding place as a means of camouflage and security from anyone looking to pillage it or the temple it resides in."

"So, you are saying that this oasis is a mirage?" the Northern king asked, still struggling to comprehend his agent's words.

"Not exactly, sir," K answered. "The oasis is real in the sense that it is a real depression in the land and it holds real water in this dry, arid region. The oasis is supplied with water through magic though. That is why the oasis never goes dry. Its purpose is to protect and hide a tomb that lies under the sands, so the magic that created this place ensures its continued existence. If one were brave enough to dive to the pool's center, one would find the bed made of stone, not sand. And, if one were to break through that stone, then one would find themselves inside a lost burial of one of The Four and the resting place for a piece of the Ascension Armor."

This all sounded incredibly risky to the armor-clad leader. The weight of his armor would make it difficult, if not impossible, for him to swim even in the shallow depths of the oasis. If this were a trap, then the paranoid leader might not be able to resurface under his armor's weight and would be rather defenseless if attacked while in the water.

He needed more reassurance that K was telling the truth.

"And you expect me to dive into the waters, break through the stone layer beneath the oasis, and single-handedly recover the armor?" the suspicious leader asked his agent.

"Not exactly," K answered.

K continued his explanation.

"I have already taken the liberty of diving the waters to confirm my theory of the tomb hidden below. And, I have already broken through the stone to reveal an opening into the tomb. That is also how I confirmed the oasis's magical foundation."

"'Magical foundation'?" asked K's master.

"Yes, when I destroyed the stone beneath the pool, the water did not drain into the tomb below. There is a magical force that keeps the water suspended above the tomb, even when there is a hole in the tomb's ceiling."

"I see," replied the still skeptical leader.

"And," he continued, "if you have done so much already, then why have you not acquired the armor already? Why wait for me to arrive and expect me to acquire the item? You could have just as easily obtained it and just handed it to me."

The hooded K crossed his arms across his chest, obviously insulted by his master's distrusting tone and questions.

"Do you not remember the effect of the tomb which once held the sword that now hangs by your side? I did not dare to enter the tomb and suffer a similar fate. But, now that I have broken the tomb's seal, it should be safe for you to enter and obtain the treasure within," K replied with a tone of sarcasm and defiance in his voice.

The hooded agent's words brought forth a flood of memories that the armored king had long tried to forget. He remembered the madness that was brought on by the tomb outside Rishdel. He remembered the constant and incoherent babbling. He even remembered how he and his friend had ventured to find the tomb together, only for him to betray and murder his friend.

K's awareness of the powerful curse that protected the tomb was both reassuring but concerning to the self-appointed king. K's explanation implied that he had done all that was necessary for someone else to safely enter the tomb and obtain the prize inside. That was the assuring part. The concerning part was that Macadre's leader had no way of knowing if K had already entered the tomb or not, or whether this was just some ploy by a corrupt mind to kill any competition for the armor.

It was said that when The Four were alive and possessed the armor pieces, they grew suspicious of one another and often said that the others each conspired to take whatever armor that individual possessed. That paranoia and mistrust was the motivating factor behind the division between the races, the racial segregation, and hatred that existed to this day. Generation after generation were told stories about how the other races were out to get them and their race's nobility so that what they had could satisfy the greed of the others. That 'greed' was usually forgotten when it came to traveling merchants who peddled wares that could not be found except through trade with the other cities and races. But even that took time to re-establish, and the merchants of other races were often watched closely by the guards of whatever city they found themselves in. There were occasional reports of harassment by the guards or city residents to the city leaders, but such reports were often dismissed as 'lies perpetrated by outsiders to discredit our people in an attempt to substantiate their own recent price increases' by the powers-that-be in each city.

Regardless of the armor's history of causing suspicion of others and K's master's current suspicion of his own agent, the hidden figure had little other choice but to descend into the pool's depths to check for the tomb said to lie beneath it and for the relic assumed to lie within its walls. He could not trust anyone else to recover the armor because there was no guarantee that they would turn over such a powerful item without a fight and he was not willing to risk his life and authority on the weak will of a subordinate. And, if K was honest, K had broken the tomb's protective seal which would not allow him to enter the tomb without going insane. With K unable to enter the tomb and the masked leader unable to trust anyone else, there was little else to do but dive in.

"Very well," he said after a moment of reflection on the armor's history, his previous experience with the other tomb, and K's reminder of what happened before. "I will go and retrieve what is mine. Remain here and ensure my safe return."

K acknowledged his master's command and took his position on the edge of the water while he watched his king wade off into the shallow waters of the oasis, but not before handing his master some much-needed supplies that would be necessary to complete his task.

The leader and his heavy armor moved slowly in the water. With each step, the water splashed about and sent several small waves across the water's surface. Each step took the armored individual deeper as he got nearer the pool's center. The oasis was shallower than expected. The water reached only to the bottom of his chin as the armored person stood near the opening under the oasis. The hole through the stone ceiling could easily be seen through the crystal-clear water that filled the oasis.

K's retelling of his efforts seemed to be confirmed, as the water hovered over the opening but did not drain into the space below. In fact, the water did not extend down to the stone. Instead, the bottom of the oasis seemed to stop about an inch or so above the stone roof. There was obviously some magical effect at play in keeping the water suspended above the tomb and the makeshift entrance.

Making use of the supplies K had handed him earlier, the masked leader dropped a rope into the water and through the hole. The rope had been tied to one of the trees surrounding the oasis, and the two hoped that the tree and rope would support the weight of the armor that the leader had refused to take off.

He took a deep breath from under his mask and dropped down into the water. K watched from the pool's edge as his master slid down the rope and disappeared into the tomb.

***

Inside the tomb, the wet armor dripped onto the dry, stone floor. The armor's bearer looked up through the hole that he had just climbed down. The water shimmered above as he just stared in awe at the magic's power to lock the forces of nature in that persistent state. A small sliver of light shone through the hole ever so slightly, thanks to the day's end rapidly approaching.

Beyond the small amount of light that penetrated the opening above, the tomb was completely dark. Even the floor tiles beneath the feet of the tomb's intruder could barely be seen in the fading illumination from above. This too was something that K had apparently predicted, as the unknown leader pulled from a pouch K had handed him a torch that had been wrapped in animal skins to help keep it dry in the oasis's waters, along with some pieces of flint to help him light the torch.

The light from above was beginning to fade more and more as night took over at the surface. The armor-clad leader worked quickly to strike the flint and spark the torch's flame to life. The light of the torch's fire pushed back the darkness that filled the tomb, but just barely. He struggled to see more than a few feet in front of himself, as the opaque blackness seemed to fight against the light emanating from his flaming torch.

He stretched his arm up as high as he could to force the torch's light up towards the ceiling. Under the dim light that made its way through the darkness, shiny spots could be seen dotting the tomb's roof. He quickly returned to the fractured stone on the floor, which K had broken to make an entrance into the tomb, to see if he could better understand the shining source. Luckily, the torch's light was more effective when he could get it closer to the stone on the floor, which he could now see was granite, and the light revealed that the ceiling was decorated with gemstones that sparkled and shined in what little light that permeated the darkness.

His immediate reaction was to pry the gems from the stones, but he quickly thought better of it.

"Bah, I am not here for trinkets and baubles, I come for a much greater prize," he thought to himself as his monetary greed was quickly overcome by his greed for the power that he felt the Ascension Armor could procure for him, once in his possession.

He stood up and proceeded to walk about the tomb, inspecting every nook and cranny with his torch. The walls were covered in runes and an unusual language. Eventually, he found a carved relief that revealed who the tomb was built for and what prize it might hold.

The relief depicted a mighty dwarf warrior defending himself and a large pile of gold or coins from a horde of dragons. It was obvious that this was the tomb of Trylon, the dwarven king. And, this meant the tomb held Trylon's breastplate, said to be virtually weightless despite being made of solid metal made from the glowing ore. The only problem was that there was no sign of the glowing relic in the tomb.

The intruder scanned the tomb but saw nothing that glowed with the blue glow similar to his sword. He even unsheathed his sword at one point to make sure that his sword still glowed in the tomb's darkness and that there was not some magic that suppressed that characteristic. The sword glowed as it always had, and this perplexed its owner.

"If I am the first to enter this tomb, then it should be here," he thought to himself.

He continued to search the tomb before he stumbled across a smooth wall with no inscriptions, runes, or other carvings. This seemed very odd and out of place among the other walls that were covered in intricate and detailed carvings. The sword-wielding tomb raider was left to surmise that this was a false wall and something must be hidden behind it.

Without hesitation, he drew his sword and began hacking and chopping at the stone wall. Normally, such an act would ruin a blade, but as the sparks flew, the blade remained undamaged, without even a scratch. With each strike, the stone wall began to chip away as the sword's razor-sharp edge dug in like no other sword was capable of doing.

It took several minutes of work before the hard, polished granite stone began to crumble away in larger and larger chunks. Eventually, a small hole formed in the stone, proving that the wall hid another opening in the tomb's interior.

A blue light could be seen flooding out from the hole. This could mean only one thing to the lusting tomb robber, that the breastplate of Trylon was just behind this stone. The thought of recovering the breastplate and adding to his power filled him with excitement and anticipation. He immediately began using the pommel of his sword to smash away the remaining stone until there was an opening big enough for him to squeeze into the armor's resting place.

As he pushed his way through the narrowing opening in the false wall, the blue glow faded in the torchlight that began to fill the space. The breastplate of Trylon rested on a stand, just waiting for him to take it. He walked up to the breastplate and easily lifted it from its centuries-old resting place with a single hand. The legends about the armor's weight were confirmed. The only thing that caught the breastplate's new owner by surprise was the armor's construction.

The breastplate appeared to be one single piece with a large opening at the bottom and some openings at the top for someone's head and arms to go. The armor did not appear to be adjustable or hinged like most breastplates so that they could easily be fit to a wearer whose size might change over time. No, this armor seemed fitted to a single wearer. This puzzled its new owner. How could he use the breastplate in his conquest if he could not wear it?

He figured that perhaps that mystery could be solved later, and that now, he needed to return to the surface and await the arrival of his troops, who should be headed to the oasis.

No longer having a need for the torch, he dropped the lit torch on the ground and walked with the weightless breastplate in hand, using its blue glow to light the way through the tomb and back to the rope hanging through the ceiling. He then used his belt to strap the breastplate to his hip by feeding the leather belt through the opening for his neck and out one of the openings for his arms. It made for an awkward attachment, thanks to the item's bulk and design, but he had little other means to carry it from the tomb. He had hoped to don whatever armor he found in the tomb and simply wear it out, but the breastplate's size seemingly foiled that plan.

Using what strength remained in his arms after two long days of riding and chopping his way through the fake stone wall of the tomb, he hoisted himself up the rope, mostly by pure adrenaline and joy. As he reached the top of the tomb, he took a deep breath and pulled himself onto the top of the tomb and into the depths of the oasis.

He struggled to work his body through the hole with his new prize so clumsily attached to his waist. It took him much longer to get out of the tomb than it had for him to get in it, and as such, he was quickly running out of air and desperate to stand up. Finally, he was able to free the breastplate from the stone it clung to, and this allowed him to stand up straight again. The water was still up to his chin, but that was okay because this meant he was able to breathe once more.

With his lungs full of air once more and his prize strapped to his hip, the proud thief made his way back to shore.

Seeing the green breastplate and its familiar, faint blue glow hanging from his master's belt in the growing darkness of night, K grew curious.

"Why aren't you wearing your prize?" K asked.

"Are you kidding?" K's master shouted back rather angrily.

"This thing will never fit me. I will have to have one of my smiths try to modify it for me," he added.

K just laughed at his master's ignorance before educating him on another of the armor's secrets.

"There's no need to modify it. The Breastplate of Trylon will adapt itself to its wearer," K explained. "Just slip your arms up from the bottom, through the openings on the side, and pull the armor down over your head. The breastplate will expand or shrink to fit all who wear it. Its makers crafted the armor for a hero in his prime but knew well that as he aged his physique might change, and that there was always the possibility that the armor would be passed down to a successor, such as yourself, who might be differently proportioned compared to Trylon."

This seemed rather odd to the breastplate's new owner, but K had been right about everything else up to this point so there was little reason to doubt him now. He quickly removed the shimmering green breastplate from his belt before unfastening and removing his current traditional breastplate. As he started to put his arms through it as K had described, he soon realized that his masked helmet was making it difficult for him to move about the way he needed and would be forced to take his helmet off, something that he had not done in front of anyone else in some time.

He turned his back to K and slowly pulled the masked helmet from his head while being careful to keep his face hidden from K or any other would-be onlookers in the area. He was even careful to make sure that his face's reflection could not be seen on the nearby water's surface.

K discreetly glanced at his exposed master's head, but all he saw was the chainmail coif that covered his head under the helmet. No real details could be seen from K's current vantage point, but he did not dare move and risk the wrath of his master.

Not wanting his identity exposed any longer than necessary, Macadre's king quickly put his arms through the openings, lifted the breastplate over his head, and pulled it down towards his body as K had explained. The breastplate did exactly as K had said it would. The ore seemed to pull apart and stretch around his body as the anonymous king levered his arms down, pulling the breastplate to his hips. Once he arms were at his side, the breastplate made a clicking sound as it formed around his frame. The solid shell of armor now fully encompassed his torso, with the joints and pivot points in the right place to allow him to move properly. Also, the armor managed to retain the same weightlessness it had at its former size. It was a most impressive feat, to be sure, and one that left its new bearer stumped about how such things could be possible.

Astonished by the breastplate's ability to grow to his size, the unmasked leader almost forgot about his missing headpiece. He started to turn back to K when he caught his face's reflection in the water. It was the first time in a long time that he saw his piercing steel blue eyes and a hint of the blonde hair that hid beneath the coif. He quickly remembered his helmet and mask and spun back around to face away from K until his cover was once more fully intact.

Chapter 6

As morning came for Riorik and the others, all seemed calm.

Each member of the group took their turn at watch, but none saw anything of interest or concern. The night had been quiet, well, except for Wuffred's snoring that had seemed to get worse after moving through the hayfields outside Tyleco.

The group sat around their bedrolls eating simple breakfast sandwiches made from some of the fresh bread and cured meats Wuffred had purchased at the market in Tyleco, days before. For the three Rangers, this was the first fresh goods they had obtained since leaving Rishdel, after Riorik and Nordahs were ordered to kill Wuffred but instead chose to spare their friend's life and live a life of exile away from the other elves.

The four friends discussed how unexciting their watch had been throughout the night. It was a contest between them to see who had the least boring watch. They laughed as each took turns trying to describe the lack of events in the most exciting way possible.

"I stared out into the inky blackness before me," Nordahs started on his description about his watch, "and the night stared back at me. I was surrounded by the watchful eyes of the night and its minions. Lesser elves would have found themselves too scared to move, but I am no average elf. No, I am something else. I readied my sword for battle and charged at the night. Its presence was overwhelming compared to my own, but a hero like me does not fade when faced with a larger opponent. Nay, a hero like me rises to the challenge and rise I did. Our weapons locked in combat, and we fought one another for the entirety of my watch as I refused to let its evil swallow my friends in their sleep. The night and I were in a state of constant back and forth as I drove my blade's edge deep into the darkness, only to find that the more I cut off an endless supply simply filled the void. However, in the end, the darkness grew tired, knowing it could not best me and began to retreat. Confident that I had successfully repelled my foe and defended my defenseless friends still deep in their slumber, I woke up Ammudien and told him it was his turn to take watch. The end."

The others giggled and laughed at his story while he stood up and took a quick bow before his audience.

Riorik went next.

"As darkness fell across the land, a sense of evil filled the air. As a well-trained and experienced Ranger, I have been taught to never let my guard down and to always be aware of the ever-present danger that surrounds us, just waiting for an opportunity to strike. I leaned down closer to the ground and used my highly honed sense of hearing to discover the voices of our enemies planning their attack. The chitter and squeaks of the nightlife could be heard conspiring against us. Luckily for you, my sleeping allies, I uncovered their plot to sneak into our camp under the cover of night and steal our food. Using my superior stealth, I was able to stalk our enemies, making them my prey instead of the other way around. One of their advance reconnaissance members made a dash for the campsite, hoping to slip past my watchful eye, but their attempt to evade me failed. I followed the furry would-be food thief until they reached their target. I wanted them to think they had succeeded. Just as it began to chew its way into our bag with its razor-like teeth, I smacked the over-grown rat on the tail with the flat of my blade. The foul beast squealed in terror before fleeing the camp. I could hear how he told the others of my legendary skills and warned them off from making additional attempts at our goods."

Another round of laughs and applause followed as Riorik also bowed, but he embellished his bow by adding an elegant hand gesture.

Wuffred, lacking the level of imagination and storytelling skills that his elven friends clearly possessed, decided he would try telling a story next.

"So, off in the distance, I heard a howl. The war-cry of an approaching wolf pack? Perhaps, but I'd be damned if a wolf or wolves would tear your throats out on my watch. I grabbed my sword and stood at the ready to face off against the hairy animals if they came over here. But, they never came, so I ended up just holding my sword all night for no reason."

The others giggled, mostly out of pity. Wuffred gave a stiff bow, slightly embarrassed at what he knew to be a poor story compared to those of his friends, but at least he was brave enough to try.

Next, it was Ammudien's turn as the others looked to see what fanciful story the mage might spin. But, being the ever-logical gnome, his story was more factual and less fanciful.

"Unlike you all," Ammudien started, "I did not face off against harmless rodents or the non-threatening sense of night.

Instead, I turned my attention to the large mass that camped behind us. While you three danced about against imaginary enemies and slept, I focused my magic on what really lurked in the shadows. I was determined to figure out if it was anything of danger to us or what its intentions might be, but, like before, my attempts to identify it failed. Despite the carrying on you three apparently did during your time at watch and Wuffred's infernal snoring, whatever lay in the grass along our path did not move. It was either dead or sleeping very heavily. All I know is that nothing else stirred during my watch and that we still do not know what it is that hides just over there."

The seriousness of his voice did not prompt any giggles or applause. No, it was a stark reminder to the others that they may have been under a very real threat the entire night, despite their lighthearted stories. And, now that daybreak had come, there was an opportunity to suss out exactly what was there.

"So, does this mean that we should backtrack to where that thing lies to figure out what it is?" Nordahs asked, after taking some time to process Ammudien's story.

Wuffred, still determined to complete their quest quickly so that he could return to Asbin, was quick to offer his opinion on the matter.

"I say no," he answered. "I say we continue forward. If we have a stalker, then Ammudien will sense its presence following us. I see no reason for us to lose time making our way to the next relic just to identify an animal that may have just happened to wander across our path. Until we know that we are being followed, we should forge ahead."

"I agree with Wuffred," Riorik said, concurring with his human friend's plan.

Having recently acquired two of the four missing armor pieces, Riorik was also eager to move on to the next temple. He still had not figured out how finding the armor might lead him to the truth about his father, but he still strongly felt that there was a strong connection between the armor and Cyrel's disappearance.

The group knew that they were still a good distance away from their target destination, so they soon agreed it was ultimately better to make progress towards their objective instead of going backward without good cause. They packed up their campsite and promptly headed off towards whatever tomb Ammudien's magic had found the day before. It was going to be a full day's hike before they got there.

***

The laughter and commotion coming from the campsite woke Captain Cooper. The previous day was long, and the weary captain slept hard through the night. If it had not been for the noise of his prey, then he might have slept through their upcoming departure.

Luckily for the captain, unlike those he pursued, Captain Cooper did not have any goods or materials to pack before he was ready to leave his night's accommodations. He was also lucky in the fact that he was a man who was known to snack, so he kept various jerked meats and candies in his pouches to nibble on throughout the day. This meant that the dogged guard would not have to forfeit his pursuit for a lack of food.

The captain withdrew a long stick of dried meat from a pouch and proceeded to gnaw at it while he sat in a crouched position, watching his prey from a distance. His teeth worked the thick, leathery meal until it was soft enough to rip a piece away from the rest. He sat there chewing the salty meat like a cow chews its cud. He watched as the distant figures moved about gathering their goods. He even remained in his position after they set off, continuing in a straight line on the same northeasterly direction they had before.

The patient human waited until the group had moved almost beyond his sight, which was much better during the day than it had been in the night. Just as Wuffred and the others began to become little more than specks on the horizon, Captain

Cooper slowly followed after them. He wanted to try and keep as much distance between himself and Wuffred as possible in the daylight.

"If I can see them, then they can surely see me," he thought to himself as a rationalization to his strategy.

He carefully followed the group throughout the day. There were several times that the group would stop, suddenly forcing Captain Cooper to move to cover. Sometimes that was easier said than done, as there were vast open areas the group crossed in their relentless endeavor to reach wherever they were headed. Sometimes he would get lucky and find a tree or a large rock. Other times he would take his chances at trying to mask his presence behind fence posts or in clumps of tall grass that sprouted randomly across the landscape.

It was not an easy chase, but it was one Captain Cooper was determined to see through to the end.

But, the captain could not help but think about his wife and family that he left behind in Tyleco. Most days he was home in time for dinner and would play with his two children before putting them to bed. Captain Cooper was a loving family man, but in his haste, he left Tyleco without notifying anyone, never expecting to have gone so far from home to discover Wuffred's truth. His thoughts drifted to what his wife's thoughts were.

"Surely someone saw me leave the gates and would have told her, but my current whereabouts and motives would remain unknown. Does she think I left her and our family? Would she think I left to have an illicit meeting with someone else? Does the fact that I have not returned make her think I am dead?"

The many theories and thoughts raced through his mind, but he knew he would never be able to answer them until he returned to Tyleco. It was certainly the foundations for strong emotions to return home, but he could not shake the feeling that Wuffred's lies and current path spelled danger for Tyleco and its inhabitants, including his family. Captain Cooper was compelled to uncover the truth to protect the city and people he loved.

Over the course of the morning, Captain Cooper successfully followed the group and appeared to have remained undetected. But, it was at midday that he began to worry.

The group he had been following stopped just shy of the border that ran between the Narsdin and Heilstur regions, as well as the border that ran between the Heilstur and Ellias regions. This area of connecting borderlines represented the extreme boundary of Captain Cooper's authority but was also a key trail for smugglers and bandits looking for passage into the northern area, where it was often easier to sell stolen goods. This fact raised the obvious questions in the city guard captain's mind regarding Wuffred's true identity.

"I knew it," Captain Cooper thought, "he's nothing more than a common criminal. That explains the odd company he keeps. They must all be thieves trying to get back to Nectana."

He stewed in anger at Wuffred's presumed background, but his attention was quickly pulled back from his thoughts and towards the group he followed. There was a bright flash that came from where the group sat that was most unexpected by Captain Cooper.

"What was that?" he wondered to himself. "Are they signaling others? Is that some sort of trap?"

He did not know the cause of the light burst, but the reality was the light came from Ammudien. The gnome had checked their direction towards the next tomb, and the spell caused the radiant burst of light. Whatever the source, Captain Cooper's attention was once more fully on the group he had followed for so long. As such, he continued to watch as the smallest member of the group walked away from the others and seemed to head in the captain's direction. Captain Cooper began to get nervous, and he prepared to defend himself if necessary. But, the need to defend his position never came. The small figure stopped well shy of the captain's location, but what he observed next was unlike anything he had ever seen before.

The individual appeared to couch down, and a strange glowing light could be seen surrounding the small person's hands. The sight somewhat scared the veteran soldier, but his eyes remained fixed on the unbelievable events unfolding before him. He was careful not to make a move and alert his prey or disrupt the unusual ritual being conducted in front of him. After a few short seconds, the strange glowing light that had enveloped the figure's hands disappeared as the person quickly stood up, looked directly in Captain Cooper's direction, and ran back to the others.

***

"We ARE being followed!" Ammudien exclaimed as he ran back to the others.

"Are you certain?" Riorik asked.

"Positive," Ammudien replied. "When I cast my detection spell, I felt the same disturbance as before some distance away. It's too far for me to see directly, but I definitely detected a similar presence. And, whatever it is, it is directly on the same path that we walked again. There is little doubt in my mind that the strange presence is following us."

"We must confront it and finally figure out exactly who or what it is," suggested Nordahs.

The elf was not thrilled at the prospect of an unknown force stalking them. However, Wuffred was still focused on moving to the next target, so his suggestion was somewhat contrary to his friend's opinion.

"It hasn't bothered us yet, so there is no reason to think that it means us any harm. It made no attempt to attack in the night and remains at a distance from us. I say we leave it be and continue on our quest," the human recommended.

The group immediately looked towards Riorik for his thoughts. The young elf was the group's de facto leader, so in times of contradiction, like the current one, it usually fell to Riorik to make the final decision.

Riorik took several minutes of contemplation as he weighed his options and the risks associated with each. Eventually, he came to a decision and was prepared to tell his friends.

"I say we move on," he started. "Whatever is trailing behind us is staying at a distance too great for even our elven eyes, so it obviously does not want to be seen. We know nothing about what might be a very dangerous foe, and I do not want to risk injury or death for any one of us with us being so close to another piece of the armor. For all we know, it could just be a curious farmer or something that finds our group intriguing."

"But what happens when we get to the next tomb and that thing is still following us?" a very concerned Nordahs asked, after hearing his friend's conflicting thoughts on the subject.

"We'll address it only if and when it demands it," Riorik answered. "I don't think a single entity will pose that great of a threat to the four of us. Just look at what happened when that stupid barbarian Whilem attacked me at the tower. Wuffred held him off, and Asbin, little ol' Asbin, bashed his face in. Surely three trained Rangers, one of which is a berserker, and highly talented mage can take care of one opponent without much trouble. We have the numbers, the training, and the upper hand in that we know it's there and following us. There is no real threat to us or our mission if we continue forward at this point."

Riorik's decision was final, and Nordahs knew that he would not be able to change his friend's opinion on the matter. The others just nodded in agreement with Riorik's decree. And with that decision made, the group continued in the direction Ammudien's last check confirmed as the right way towards the next tomb.

They moved with purpose towards their destination, with Riorik and Nordahs keeping a cautious eye on what was behind them but never able to really make it out. Their stalker was being careful to stay out of sight, but it did not faze the group. And, as the day turned to night, Riorik was encouraged as his keen eyesight spied what looked to be an oasis just off in the distance ahead of them.

****

Progress for the troops marching from Macadre to the oasis was slow. The supply wagons were constantly getting bogged down in the mud, causing everyone to stop and wait for them to be pulled free. Being forced to march only as fast as the slowest units in the convoy meant that the entire army moved at a snail's pace across the barren wasteland between Macadre and the mountains to the city's south. It was likely to take days for the full force to reach the oasis, even if it meant marching from daybreak until well after nightfall.

With each delay, more and more goods were offloaded from the wagons and given to individual orcs and trolls to carry. The idea was that if they could lessen the weight of the wagons, they would get buried in the soft ground less often. It was a sound idea, but the extreme softness of the water-logged soil still seemed to constantly suck the wheels of the wagons down into its gooey underbelly. It made for a long and tiring day's march for all.

It was near the day's end before the group reached the base of the mountains that their leader had passed a full two days earlier. It was only now that they realized the ease of their previous tribulations. The mountain path was narrow, much narrower than the formation they had been marching in up until this point. The troops would be forced to funnel through the mountains no more than three abreast at a time, one at a time for the larger, wider trolls and only two at a time for their slightly smaller orc cousins. The wagons would barely fit in the width of the path, and if one had an issue, there would be no room to maneuver around it or salvage it should it fall from the path's edge.

This meant that it would take considerable time to get their master's full army through the mountain pass. The one advantage they had was that the weather had improved much since their leader's passage through the mountains. The steep, rocky paths had dried up considerably, making it easier for the army's volume to flow along its trails, but it was still not without risk. Rockslides, washouts, and paths that spanned the small gorge would still pose a very real threat at all times until they reached the safety of the other side.

Not wanting to start their passage attempt across such a perilous path so late in the day, the decision was made to make camp for the night. The generals concluded that their troops would need the full light of day to survive their passage across the mountains. Their leader had made the journey at night, as did

Grue and his troops of gnolls and orc at the even more dangerous pass near Nectana, but the generals were afraid to make the pass at night so that was their justification.

Chapter 7

In the dim light under the stars, Wuffred, Riorik, Nordahs, Ammudien, and their unseen follower approached nearer the oasis. The sharp-eyed elves could see the trees that lined the sandy, water-filled depression that sat alone in the barren landscape that surrounded it. But, the thing that stood out most to them was not the source of fresh water but the fire that burned just at its edge. The red flames of the fire shined brightly against the dark blue background of the night on the horizon. It was an unexpected sight in such a desolate environment and filled the elves with concern.

"Do you think it's another bandit camp?" Nordahs asked Riorik as the two kept a close watch.

"Hard to say from here," Riorik replied.

The elves had only seen the shadowy figures of two people moving about around the fire, but that did not mean that they were the only ones there. For all the rangers knew, the camp could be full of people who were sleeping and not visible from that distance or angle.

"There isn't much cover, from the looks of it, and the daytime can be pretty brutal in a landscape like this, so the absence of buildings and tents tells me that whoever is there doesn't plan to stay long. Perhaps defectors from Kern or maybe prisoners who escaped the guards?" Riorik postulated.

"We could always have Ammudien do his thing and find out," Nordahs reminded his friend.

Always eager not to rush into a fight, Riorik quickly agreed with that plan and waved for Ammudien to come to their position.

"We need you to hide behind this dune and use your spell to see how many people are at that watering hole," Riorik explained to the mage.

"Why behind the dune?" Ammudien asked out of curiosity, feeling it was a strange detail in the elf's request.

"Easy," Riorik said, "I want to make sure they don't see you, and when you cast that spell your hands light up like a torch basically. We need to know how many are over there, not tell them that we are over here."

Riorik's logic was sound. The spell did cast a light, albeit a faint one, and if the elves could see the campfire from their current position, then there was a possibility that whoever was at the oasis might see Ammudien's spell while it was in use.

"Sounds reasonable to me," Ammudien replied.

Ammudien stepped up behind the dune and checked to make sure that he was completely shielded from the oasis. Satisfied that the light from his spell would not be easily detected, he looked back at Riorik and Nordahs who were still standing unusually close to the gnome. He gave them a look to suggest they move, but the elves missed the meaning of his subtle gesture.

"Shoo," he finally whispered as he waved his hands at them.

This time they understood and quickly took several steps back from their mage friend.

As he had done so many times before, the gnome mage knelt to the ground and cast his spell. He sat for several seconds as he focused on the different ripples, making sure to consider the ripples of his friends as always. Once he was done, Ammudien stood up and waved for the others to join him, similar to how they had summoned him just moments before. He just stood there staring at his friends with a grimace on his face.

"Let me guess, 'good news, bad news'?" Riorik asked rhetorically.

"Yup," the gnome answered, "as it always seems to be."

"Alright then, out with it," Riorik requested.

"The good news is that there appears to be only two figures near the fire," Ammudien led.

"And the bad news?" Nordahs asked.

"We still have our 'friend' following us. Whatever, or whoever, seems to still be intentionally keeping a healthy distance from us, but there is no question that it is still there," the mage answered.

The news was both encouraging and annoying. With only two people at the oasis, Riorik felt comfortable either waiting for them to leave the area or overpowering them if it came down to it. It was the persistent presence of this unknown force following them that made him uneasy. He still felt confident that a single predator offered little threat to their group, but if this unknown party was in cahoots with the people at the oasis, then it could be something entirely more problematic for them.

What was worse, the group did not know for sure just how close or far they were from the next tomb Ammudien's magic had detected earlier in the day and knowing that there were others nearby made it too dangerous to cast that spell again. The extreme brightness that the spell emitted would surely catch the attention of anyone in the area and pinpoint exactly where Riorik and the others were camped.

Riorik decided that he needed to know more about what was going on at the oasis. If he could move a little closer to where the unknown duo was camped, perhaps he could figure out who they were, what kind of threat they might pose, and how long they might plan to stay camped there. He discussed his plans with the others, and they were not thrilled by his proposition. The others thought it too risky for Riorik to approach on his own. Two against one was not good odds, they explained.

"If any of us are to approach, then it should be all of us, together, as a team," Ammudien said.

Wuffred and Nordahs expressed their agreement with their gnome friend's sentiment.

"If there's a fight, then we should fight as a group. We're stronger together than apart," Nordahs said convincingly.

Riorik looked at the faces of his companions and immediately knew that their determination matched his own. There was no chance the elf would be allowed to attempt such a risky mission on his own. It was all or nothing on this trip and he knew it.

"Alright," he agreed, "we do it together then."

Ammudien came up with a quick strategy that he shared with the team before setting off.

"Let me take the lead," the gnome started. "With my smaller size, I will be harder to see. My eyes may not be as sharp in the darkness as you elves, but I create a much smaller shadow and presence. Then, behind me by some several feet, the two elves follow. This will allow your superior eyes to get a good look while reducing your chance to be seen, since I will be the forward lookout. And lastly, Wuffred, you can follow behind Riorik and Nordahs. Nothing personal, my big friend, but your larger frame and poor eyesight in these conditions are not ideal, so we need you to stay at the back while we scout out the oasis. If there is trouble, then come running for sure, but you cast a big shadow and despite your Ranger training you are still not as stealthy as the three of us."

Wuffred knew the gnome was right about his inferior abilities compared to his friends, so he made no attempt to argue with Ammudien's plan or dispute the mage's claims. Nordahs also agreed to the plan. He did not want Riorik to go alone in case there was trouble, but the young elf did not want to take the lead on this scouting mission. The only one to offer a different option was Riorik, of course.

"I'd like to make an alternate suggestion," Riorik said.

Nordahs just dropped his head. He knew what his friend was thinking, and it was not something Nordahs was particularly fond of doing at this late hour. Wuffred just shook his head. The human just wanted to get it over with, but the more time the others spent talking about it, the longer it would take him to return to Asbin and their unborn child. Ammudien just looked at Riorik with an annoyed look on his face. The gnome did not like having others challenge his solutions because he felt his gnome mind was superior and therefore so were his plans.

Riorik offered his plan to the group, despite the obvious reluctance demonstrated by the others through their facial expressions.

"What if we split into two groups?" he started. "Nordahs and I can sweep around to the opposite side of the oasis. With our stealth and keen eyesight, we should still be able to observe the area from even that distance under the night sky. While we are doing that, Ammudien, you approach from this side of their location. Your small size and stealth will allow you to approach close without detection. Close enough that your eyes can confirm

what ours see. We take a quick look to see what's there and then
we regroup here to share what we learned."

Wuffred instantly noticed that his name was not included
in Riorik's plan.

"Umm, what about me, Riorik?" he asked curiously.

"Your job is to stay here and protect our back and our
camp," Riorik answered.

Wuffred was not pleased with Riorik's answer. He felt the
elf did not want to say it but felt that the human lacked their
ability to be stealthy, which was partly true, or that he was simply
a liability. The berserker raised his finger and opened his mouth
to protest, but before he could say a single word, Riorik
interrupted him.

"We still don't know what it is that follows us. If we move
off to check out this other camp, we need to make sure whatever
that is doesn't come here and ruin this camp for us. We need a
place to return to, and there is nobody better equipped to defend
what is essentially our base from an unknown threat than you. We
need you to protect us from whatever that is."

Riorik's words immediately calmed Wuffred's frustration.
It made sense. Wuffred was not as stealthy as the others, his eyes
could not see as well in the dark as the others, but his strength
was better than the others, so when it came to mounting a single-

person defense against an unknown assailant, he was the obvious choice. It did not take long for Wuffred to agree with Riorik's point of view on the subject.

"Well, that makes sense," Wuffred happily agreed with the perceived admission from Riorik that he was indeed the strongest member of the team.

The fact was that even when he was not in a berserked state, Wuffred was physically the strongest person in the group, but the agility of the elves made them formidable opponents that could often outmaneuver his brute force, something that was repeatedly made evident back in their days of training at the Rangers Guild in Rishdel. Nobody in the group ever questioned Wuffred's power, but it was nice for the human to hear those words from his friends every once in a while. His ego had taken a beating over the years of exclusion from other humans and even from the years of being treated like he was something less than a person at the hands of the elven elders that took him in after being banished from his home.

Wuffred's ego aside, the plan had been set and everyone was finally on board. Each party member knew their role and route. Wuffred's was obviously the easiest, so the group set about to learn more about the mystery campers near the oasis.

***

Ammudien, having the shortest distance to cover of the three scouts, came up to the side of the unwitting campers after a few brief minutes of sneaky maneuvering. The small mage finally stopped as he crested the top of a sand dune and could clearly see into the small campsite in the clearing below. He had not expected to have such a clear vision into the campsite so quickly, so his little feet scampered to halt his advance and put him back on the other side of the mound of sand.

The gnome dropped to the ground quickly to avoid being seen by the camp's two occupants. Only the top of his hooded head could be seen poking over the top of the sandy mound that supported him. There was also a quick realization that he needed to keep his movements to a minimum as the sands beneath rolled away and down towards his unsuspecting targets.

The darkness of night was far from pitch black, with the moon's light filling the wide-open area with a soft blue light. Not enough light to see far or with much detail but still enough light for Ammudien's head to cast a visible silhouette to any nearby onlookers. Still, he held his position and observed the camp and its occupants.

The mage was surprised at what he saw. One of the occupants wore the robe of a mage, but in the blue-ish light of the night, it was too difficult for Ammudien to see what school of magic colors was represented on the cuffs and collar of the robe. Ammudien had not heard any stories about mages in this area, but then again, he had been away from Mechii for a long time now. For all the gnome knew, this mage had been sent to find him. One thing was certain to Ammudien though, the mage below certainly could not be looking for the armor too. After all, Ammudien had been virtually laughed out of the mage school for his beliefs in the armor's existence.

Even more surprising to the gnome than the robes of another mage was the camp's second occupant. This individual was wearing a lot of armor, definitely someone prepared for a fight. But more than that, the breastplate worn by this individual appeared to put off a very slight glow. Ammudien struggled to determine if the glow was just a reflection of the night's light, a reflection of the camp's fire, or the all-telling glow of the Ascension Armor. It certainly captured Ammudien's attention, but he ultimately surmised that it was just a reflection of the night's light and that his mind was jumping to wild conclusions in his exhaustion.

This curiosity was soon replaced when Ammudien turned his attention back to the robed individual. Ammudien noticed that the figure was roughly the same size as the armored person, which was odd. Gnomes made up nearly the entire population of mages with only a few other mages ever belonging to another race, but whoever Ammudien was seeing at the campsite was certainly too tall to be a gnome. In fact, the robed individual looked to be nearly the same height as the heavily armored person on the opposite side of the camp.

"This must be someone pretending to be a mage," he thought to himself, as he was certain this person could not be a real mage.

His thoughts immediately began spewing out theories about the pair. They were children simply playing dress-up. Actors trying to get into character for an upcoming performance. Rogues dressed to scare and intimidate their targets into thinking they had more power than just two common bandits. Members of a foreign army performing advanced scouting for an upcoming invasion.

Each scenario seemed ludicrous to the rational gnome, but he could not help but think there was something odd yet important about the pair in front of him. He knew that others were obviously in pursuit of the armor pieces like them, but this pair did not look like gnolls or orcs. Ammudien considered that they could be the brains behind the usually dim-witted beasts, but the lack of any signs of gnolls having been in the area left him with doubt about that connection. And, there seemed to be very little conversation between the two, so Ammudien knew only what he could see and what he might assume from that information.

The intrigued gnome observed the pair for several minutes before quietly slipping behind the cover of the sand dune and returning to the campsite where Wuffred waited.

***

Riorik and Nordahs moved quickly and silently across the soft, shifting sands. Their quick, light steps barely left an impression on the malleable material, allowing it to quickly disappear thanks to the wind that kept the sand in a perpetual state of motion. The pair moved in a straight line, with Nordahs following Riorik, careful to step in the same tracks to leave as little of a trail as possible. It took them several minutes to sweep from sand dune to sand dune before they reached the other side of the oasis while remaining hidden from view by the watering hole's current visitors.

Once they had reached the other side, the two split up. Riorik took up a position to the southeast while Nordahs moved to the northeast. This gave them each a slightly different vantage point so that their combined viewing angles allowed them to see the curious campers more fully.

Using their superior low-light viewing capabilities, the two elves were quickly able to determine that there were only two individuals at the campsite, and there did not appear to be any indications that anyone else had been at the campsite or was expected at the campsite. Only basic lodgings in the form of two simple tents could be seen, and a small campfire illuminated most of the area. One individual rested near the water's edge while the other laid on a small bedroll just outside one of the tents. At first, it seemed odd to the two Rangers that the strangers had tents but were not using them, but then again, it was a nice night out so perhaps they were just enjoying nature, something Riorik and Nordahs were often keen to do themselves.

Riorik was the first to notice the familiar robes of a mage being worn by the individual near the water. He strained and squinted, trying to identify which school of magic the mage belonged to, but the light was just too dim even for his sharp eyes to make out the exact colors. This was certainly an unexpected find to the elf, as it was for Nordahs when he finally realized what he was looking at.

The second individual was also a mystery for the elves. From Riorik's position, a palm tree partially obscured the individual, but he could make out what looked to be some type of armor being worn. This was even more confusing to Riorik than the presence of a mage or the fact that they had tents but did not sleep in them.

"That has to be uncomfortable to sleep in," Riorik thought to himself.

His leather outfit was tough but still flexible, so it was bearable to sleep in, at least most of the time, but the idea of trying to sleep in what looked like plate armor was most unpleasant in Riorik's mind.

Meanwhile, Nordahs had a much clearer view of the more distant occupant. He too noticed the individual's armored state, including how the person seemed to be clutching a sword very tightly to their chest, as if they were protecting it from something or someone. But more than that, Nordahs noticed how the armor did not seem to fully match. The breastplate, what little of it he could see, did not seem to match the style and design of the vambraces[1], gauntlets[2], greaves[3], or cuisse[4]. Usually, someone that donned a full suit of armor would have matching pieces, but the breastplate, which appeared to include the makings of the

---

[1] Vambraces - Forearm guard.
[2] Gauntlets - Armored gloves.
[3] Greaves - A piece of armor used to protect the shin.
[4] Cuisse - Plate that cover the thighs.

plackart[5], faulds[6], rerebrace[7], spaulder[8], and besagew[9], stood out in contrast to the other components. This immediately made Nordahs question the authenticity and capabilities of the armor.

"That looks like someone has cobbled together a suit of armor from bits and pieces. I'll bet that's just some thief who's just managed to steal armor here and there from some unlucky travelers and now fancies himself as a knight," Nordahs thought to himself as he reflected on what he saw.

After spending a few minutes watching the oasis and its visitors, Riorik signaled to Nordahs that it was time to rendezvous with Ammudien and Wuffred back at the campsite. The two elves slipped back into the night as quietly as they had arrived and made their way back to their friends. Ammudien had already returned by the time they made the return trip, so all that was left to do now was compare notes.

---

[5] Plackart - Extra layer of plate armor initially covering the belly.
[6] Faulds - Bands to protect the front waist and hips.
[7] Rerebrace - Plate that covers the section of upper arm from elbow to area covered by shoulder armor.
[8] Spaulder - Bands of plate that cover the shoulder and part of upper arm but not the armpit.
[9] Besagew - Circular plate that covers the armpit.

Chapter 8

Once Riorik and Nordahs returned to the camp, the young elf

went straight to Wuffred. Ammudien was eager to tell what he had seen at the oasis, but Riorik just walked right past the gnome on his way to the human. Ammudien felt somewhat insulted by Riorik's snub but chose not to say anything. Nordahs also looked on with curiosity as he watched Riorik bypass the only other person to observe the oasis.

Riorik's intentions were soon made clear to the others.

"So, Wuffred, tell me, did anything of interest happen here while we were gone? Any sign of our mystery stalker?" he asked his human friend.

Riorik was obviously curious to see if there was a connection between the pair at the oasis and whatever it was that had been following them since they left Tyleco. The elf figured that if whatever was out there was associated with the pair camped at the oasis and sensed their approach of the oasis threatened those camped there, then it might make a move to the camp or oasis to defend its allies. Wuffred's response would help him to determine if the two entities were connected in any way.

"Nope, nothing," Wuffred answered. "I saw nothing, heard nothing, noticed nothing. It was all quiet here."

There berserker's answer was telling. There did not appear to be any relationship between the two unknown groups. Whatever followed them was not part of the party currently camped at the oasis.

This revelation did little to reduce the overall threat of having at least three unidentified entities so close by. The one threat was of an unknown origin and possessed unknown capabilities and strengths. They did not know if it was a person, an animal, or something worse. Then, the oasis held two people of unknown origin, but one was dressed like a mage and the other an armored soldier.

Three against four were decent odds as Riorik and his friends still had the higher number, but not knowing the capabilities of the unknown certainly left them at a disadvantage if it turned out that they were not friendly. There was some relief in knowing that they stood a chance if it came to a fight, but a fight was not what Riorik and his friends wanted.

Confident in his theory about the lack of a relationship between the two unknown groups, Riorik finally turned his attention to Ammudien.

"And you, Ammudien, what did you see?" he finally asked the mage.

Ammudien just looked at Riorik and took a deep breath as he contemplated exactly what he wanted to say. And then, he spoke.

"I observed only two individuals from my position. The pair did not vocalize anything that was audible to me. One was dressed as a mage but is substantially taller than a gnome. I do not know of a mage that matches that description, and at the same time, I was unable to make out what mage discipline markings adorned the robe. For all I know, it could be a costume. As for the other, they wore a full suit of armor. The armor masked any signs of race or sex, but whoever wore it appeared to be of similar height to the want-to-be mage so that rules out gnome and dwarf," Ammudien said but was careful not to mention his brief thought about the glowing armor since he still felt it to be a reflection of light and not the glow of the Ascension Armor.

Riorik and Nordahs listened intently to Ammudien's description. Much of what the gnome said mirrored their own observations. However, their superior night-vision capabilities allowed them to see a few additional details that escaped the gnome's observations, either through the lack of ability or the lack of attention. Regardless, it was now their turn to share with the group.

"I was about to notice similar findings," Riorik said, confirming what Ammudien had just reported.

"From my position, I couldn't see the armored one as well, but I could see that there was someone wearing armor in the camp. I, too, noticed the tall one dressed as a mage, but sadly, in the dark, we can see but colors are not always clear. I was unable to determine the colors of the robe and cuffs. I found nothing more than Ammudien during my time observing the camp. What about you, Nord?"

All eyes turned to Nordahs, the last of the trio that spied on the campers.

"Well," he started, "most of what I saw was the same as what you two did. I saw two people camping near the water's edge and nobody else. Like the two of you, I saw what looked to be someone dressed as a mage but couldn't make out any specific colors, not that it would have meant anything to me even if I had, but still. I saw the other dressed in armor too."

Nordahs paused for a moment, and the others mistakenly assumed he was done with his story. They began to look at one another as each of them began to contemplate their options.

"However," Nordahs said, resuming his report to the surprise of the others, "the armored one was dressed funny. Most of the armor looked like it matched, but the breastplate, spaulders, and rerebraces were different. Not only were they a different design but they looked to be connected as part of a single piece of armor and not individual pieces, like in a standard suit of armor. Nor could I make out any markings on the armor that might identify what army or king its wearer might represent. The only other thing of note is that the person seemed to be clutching a sword very tightly, as if it had significant meaning or value to the holder. Perhaps it was the sword of their father or mentor, which might explain the mismatched armor?"

This additional information only seemed to add more to the mystery instead of answering the questions of who they were and whether they posed a threat. Ammudien repeated his theory that the pair might be bandits, dressed like that to spook anyone they robbed to make up for their lack of numbers. The group quickly denounced that theory on the fact that the oasis was not near any roads known to have traveling merchant traffic. Obviously, bandits would require a base out of sight for any patrols and the oasis definitely fit that bill, but it was also a great distance from roads where suitable victims could be found, which made that theory a bit less plausible.

The group continued to discuss different theories about who the two individuals at the oasis might be, but not a single theory seemed likely, as each theory was discredited by at least one of the others. It seemed destined to remain a mystery to them at this point.

And so, the decision was made to use the cover of darkness to move around the oasis along the path Riorik and Nordahs used for their scouting trip and wait out the night from the other side. Then, once the light of day provided adequate cover for Ammudien to use his magic again, the group would determine the next tomb's direction once more, in hopes that it laid beyond the oasis and out of the way of the oddly dressed unknown pair they had just observed.

***

As the first rays of the morning's light rose over the horizon, Riorik, who was on the final watch of the night, went to wake up Ammudien.

"It's time," he told his gnome friend as he gently shook the mage awake.

Ammudien instantly knew what Riorik meant. He wiped the sleep away from his eyes, as he moved away from his bed in preparation to cast his detection spell one more time. He had made sure to stay behind a large sand dune to shield the flaring light as much as he could from anyone awake at the oasis who might be watching. The mage started his search pointing away from the oasis. Their hopes would either be confirmed or dashed quickly.

As the mage's hands lit up from the spell's effect, Ammudien swept his hand back and forth away from the oasis. There was no reaction. The spell gave no indication of magic in that direction, but he continued to search, desperate to find a source that was not towards the oasis. In his mind, he knew that he would have to turn around and that the spell would find something then, but the gnome resisted the truth for as long as he could manage.

Eventually, Ammudien could not deny the truth any longer. He slowly started to turn back towards the oasis, and as if on cue, the closer his hands got to the oasis the greater the reaction became. And just as the mage had feared, the strongest reaction came when he hands directly faced the oasis and the unknown campers. The tomb was hidden near the oasis. A confrontation was now inevitable.

Ammudien only hung his head as he walked back to the others. It was immediately obvious to the others what he had found as soon as they saw his expression. It was perhaps the most disheartening feeling that any of them had felt since setting off on this grand adventure.

"The tomb is at the oasis," Ammudien said solemnly.

"Just from the look in your eyes, I figured as much," Wuffred replied slowly as he subtly shook his head.

Now the group needed to figure out how to approach the oasis with the others still there. The group spent the next several minutes discussing different plans and stories to tell if they had to interact with the unknown campers.

In the end, the group settled for a full-on surprise attack on the campsite. The hope was that a show of force may cause the two unknown individuals near the oasis to surrender without a fight, giving Riorik and the others a chance to learn more about them and what brought them to the oasis. That was a best-case scenario. The worst-case scenario was the two would feel threatened by the unannounced and imposing entrance, which would lead to a fight. Either way, the group all agreed that they needed access to the oasis to find the tomb hidden there and there was no way to do so without confronting the unknown campers. At one time, Nordahs suggested they just wait the duo out, but everyone else felt it too risky to leave someone so close to the tomb any longer than necessary to avoid risking the armor within falling into the wrong hands.

***

Captain Cooper woke up to find that his prey had moved on in the night. He was filled with fear. Fear that he had been discovered and that he was now their prey. Fear that he had lost his suspect, Wuffred, and would be forced to return to Tyleco empty-handed. Fear that without returning with proof or a captive that he would be accused of abandoning his post and either demoted or arrested. Fear that his family would suffer for his failure. His fears motivated him to press ahead and reacquire his target.

He moved as quickly as he could through the sand. His destination was where he last saw Wuffred and his friends camping. Cooper thought that he might be able to find some clues about where they might have gone. His hopes were soon dashed when he arrived at the campsite. The shifting sands had covered any signs that may have pointed him in the right direction.

The guard captain scanned the area but saw nothing with his human eyes that looked like the prey he had been hunting for so long now. But, instead of seeing Wuffred, Captain Cooper spied the palm trees that stood up in the middle of the barren sands like the beacon lights of a guard tower. He immediately understood what the trees represented and was filled with the thirst that he had resisted throughout his journey until now.

The captain quickly drew two conclusions as he made his way to the oasis. The first conclusion was that he would find cool, crisp, fresh water to satisfy his growing thirst at the heart of the oasis. The second conclusion was that he was likely to find Wuffred there, as the promise of fresh water was most certainly an irresistible draw for any other group that had been moving as he had.

He trudged his way up and down the sand dunes until he reached the last sand dune before the oasis. As he topped the last sand dune, he looked down into the depression that was the oasis. What he saw was not what he expected.

Instead of looking down to see Wuffred and his strange friends, Captain Cooper found himself staring at a hooded figure who appeared to be staring back at him. Neither individual said a word but remained with eyes locked on one another for several long seconds as each assessed the other.

Captain Cooper had seen Wuffred in the presence of a similarly robed figure before, but that person was considerably smaller than the person he was now confronted with. Was this an ally of the thief Wuffred? Captain Cooper was not sure, so he decided to ask.

"Excuse me, but have you seen…" Captain Cooper started to ask before he was interrupted by a flaming fireball flying directly at his head.

The quick-witted captain saw the incoming projectile and was able to dodge it just in time. The searing heat could be felt licking the back of his neck as it flew over him. That single act confirmed to Captain Cooper that it was indeed a mage that he saw, but the other obvious, and critical, things were that the mage had noticed him and was not friendly at all.

With his position compromised and his weapon of little value against a fire mage, Captain Cooper began to fear for his life. He was now faced with three options: charge his assailant and hope for the best, try to run back to Tyleco while dodging fireballs, or wait there to die a fiery death. And he had little time to make a choice.

Being a man of action and a man sworn to protect others, it was no surprise that Captain Cooper chose to charge the mage and face the inferno that could be unleashed. Better to die here instead of leading such a dangerous foe back to a more populated area. One life to spare thousands, he reasoned.

He took a deep breath and thought of his family, knowing it might be last time he was able to picture them in his mind. Captain Cooper quietly prayed for his family's future in the likely event of his death. Once the fight started, he knew that he would not be able to think of them, so he wanted to make sure he gave them the best farewell he could, given the circumstances.

The city guard captain drew his sword and just looked at its sharp edge as he steeled his nerves in preparation. Ready to die a soldier's death, Captain Cooper bravely stood up and began to move towards the top of the dune to face his hooded foe.

His charge was interrupted once he got back to the top of the sand dune. Captain Cooper had expected to be facing off against the mage, but instead, he found nobody. Standing still in shock, it took Captain Cooper several seconds to realize that the mage had moved closer towards the oasis and was now joined by a soldier wearing a lot of armor. The two stared off in the opposite direction at four approaching silhouettes.

Unsure of the events unfolding before him, Captain Cooper resolved to observe and then act. Not only was he tracking a suspected thief in Wuffred, but now he was also wanting to arrest the cloaked mage for assaulting a member of the city guard, even though Captain Cooper was not technically operating within the boundaries of Tyleco and Lord Veyron's authority.

All he could do now was hide and watch.

Chapter 9

Riorik, Nordahs, Wuffred, and Ammudien charged the oasis.

The four tried to be quiet in their ambush, but the effort needed to scale the sand dunes quickly made them tire faster than during their approach to the bandits camped near the ruined tower temple. It did not take long for them to start huffing and puffing, more loudly than any of them realized.

As the group topped the last dune before the oasis, it did not take long for them to realize that they had lost the element of surprise. Instead of running into a camp of unsuspecting campers who would be too afraid or shocked to fight back or resist, the two campers were not only not caught by surprise, but they were prepared for a fight.

The armored individual with the green-tinted breastplate stood at the back of the campsite, green sword in hand and poised for combat. But more worrying was the robed person who immediately began scribbling runes in the air with a wand. It was clearly a mage, and in the light of the morning, they could now see the obvious markings of a fire mage.

Fire mages were notoriously dangerous in a fight, due to the extremely volatile and destructive nature of their discipline. The only saving grace for the want-to-be heroes was the unknown mage's robes were the color of a light violet, an indication this mage's rank was only above a complete beginner. But regardless of the mage's rank, a fire mage still posed a significant threat.

The group slid to a stop in the sand at the unexpected sight. The three rangers watched with great concern to see what spell the mage was casting. They wanted to be sure-footed and ready to react, but moving in the sand made that difficult, so they had no choice but to stop and wait.

The only one of the four to not wait was Ammudien. The gnome mage stopped with his friends, but rather than wait to see what the fire mage had in store, Ammudien immediately began casting his own spell. The gnome's robes being of a golden yellow color meant that Ammudien was of greater skill and experience than the unknown fire mage. This difference in rank allowed Ammudien to cast his spell more quickly than his counterpart.

The gnome terra mage scrawled his runes into the air before flicking his wand up and in a circular motion. He was just in time, too. His spell created a swirling mass of sand to encircle the fire mage just as the fire mage finished his spell, which was apparently a fireball.

The fire mage tried to propel the fireball at the targets before the flying sand got too high but was too late. The sands blocked the fireball's path as it exploded into the floating, swirling wall. The fire spread throughout the vortex, turning what sand did not get blown away by the explosion into small shards of glass that then dropped to the ground. The fire mage's spell had missed its target but had freed the mage from the sandy prison.

Ammudien's sand shield was just the break Riorik and the others needed. They charged ahead from their position, down the sand dune, and into the camp's outer edge. As they approached, the unknown fire mage stepped forward, away from the glass circle that laid on the ground around him, before coming to a stop. The fire mage stared at the three rangers, who also stopped and stared at the aggressive mage.

Ammudien had not moved with the others. The gnome had stayed back, careful to keep his distance from the fire-flinging mage at the oasis. The terra mage did not see the value of just looking at the mage like his friends. Instead, Ammudien immediately began casting his second spell. A different set of yellow runes were quickly scribbled out, and with a flick of his wand, Ammudien drove the runes into the sand before sending them flying up into the clouds above. A thick wall of sand burst out from the ground between the mage and the three curious Rangers, dividing the two groups.

"Leave them!" shouted the armored individual still at the campsite.

The fire mage nodded at his companion's order before looking back in the direction of the gnome mage that had disrupted him earlier.

"And this one?" the raspy voice asked from under the robe's hood.

Riorik cocked his head at the fire mage's question. There was something about the cloaked figure's voice that sounded familiar to the young elf.

"That one, you can kill," came the answer from the sword-wielding figure who was now slowly advancing towards the three rangers.

***

The two mages now squared off against one another. It would be a battle of the mage disciplines. Fire versus terra. All disciplines were capable of destruction and combat, but these two schools were often considered more destructive than the others. The capacity for destruction and collateral damage in a showdown between these two mages was great, regardless of either mage's rank.

The two mages wasted no time in preparing their next spells. Ammudien used his wand to draw his runes as he always did. The gnome etched out the same yellow runes that he had before. He intended to box in his opponent. The gnome did not want to hurt the other mage, just neutralize the potential danger of the fire magic.

Meanwhile, the fire mage was using his wand to draw runes that flickered like flames as they hung in the air. The runes looked remarkably similar to Ammudien's runes. This time, the fire mage drew the runes with less finesse and more haste. The runes were less smooth, but it allowed the mage to complete the spell faster than before.

Both mages finished their runes at almost the exact same time. They both used the same flicking motion of their wands to drive the runes into the ground before sending them soaring up above their heads. The same thick sand wall that Ammudien had used to separate the mage from his friends now appeared in front of the fire mage, separating the two mages. Simultaneously to Ammudien's wall's appearance, a towering wall of fire erupted from the ground just feet in front of the gnome. Each of the mages had created barriers in front of the other, either to prevent some magic from being used or to obscure their own moves from their opponent.

Neither mage let the walls slow them down though.

The fire mage drew a simple swirl rune before shoving his wand through the center of the rune's swirl. A cone of fire erupted from the wand's tip. The intense heat from the steady flame burned and blasted a hole through the gnome's sand wall. The fire mage sustained the effect to continue tearing down the wall of soil until there was a gap big enough for the robed figure to pass through with ease. Once free, the mage immediately started on his next spell.

Ammudien, trapped behind the wall of flames, had a similar thought of escape from behind the trap.

The gnome drew a long, wavy rune the color of brown that resembled the ripples of water across a pond's surface more than anything else. Under that symbolic rune, he drew a few other runes before pushing the whole set forward with his wand. A tidal wave of sand sprang from the dune behind him and rolled forward. The sandy crest broke over the gnome's head and crashed down on the fiery wall that blocked his way. The sand covered the wall, suffocating and extinguishing the fire. As the cloud of sand and smoke cleared, Ammudien stepped forward to get a clear look at his magical foe.

It was apparent that the fire mage possessed skills higher than the robes suggested. The firewall spell and the potency it was cast with was far beyond the normal range of mages of that color. However, the mage's casting speed told the more experienced Ammudien that while the unknown mage knew spells higher than its apparent rank, that they lacked the experience to summon such magic with ease and efficiency.

With the barriers defeated, the two mages squared off again.

Unfortunately, the fire mage had escaped his barrier first and was able to complete his next spell before Ammudien. The gnome watched as the fire mage drew a new set of runes, accompanied by a series of circles that were flung up and over the gnome's head. This forced the smaller mage to abandon his current spell and transition into a more defensive posture.

The fire mage's spell had summoned a multitude of fireballs to rain down from the sky onto the gnome's position. Ammudien had to take his eyes off the fire mage as he quickly summoned and sent similar balls of sand up from the ground to intercept each plummeting ball of fire. The rate of fireballs hurdling towards him was fast, very fast. It took every second available for the speedy gnome to summon each ball of sand and throw it towards the nearest fireball. With each fireball defeated, Ammudien was falling farther and farther behind. If the fire mage's meteor shower spell did not end soon, then it was only a matter of time before Ammudien would be overwhelmed.

As the falling balls of fire got closer and closer to Ammudien and the tiny mage felt the heat from the explosions brush his face, he seemed doomed by the spell's effect. But, just as his pace of casting his defensive spells slowed beyond the point of effectiveness, the fire mage's spell ended. The terra mage had successfully outlasted the fire mage's powerful spell. However, the fire mage had been preparing his next spell while Ammudien had been fighting for his life.

The gnome looked back towards his opponent just in time to see a massive fireball flying in his direction. With no time to cast a counterspell, Ammudien was left with no choice but to try and dodge the giant flaming orb. Ammudien tucked and rolled down the sand dune, going directly under the incoming projectile. His escape was close to failure. So close in fact that when the fireball struck the sand where he had been standing and exploded, the intense heat from the explosion and the flames splashing out from its epicenter managed to catch part of the rolling mage's robes on fire. The fire was short-lived as the mage rolled away and snuffed out the flames almost instantly, but they left some singed and scorched marks on the otherwise impeccably clean garment.

The angry, nimble gnome rolled and popped up to his feet and immediately started to cast his next spell. This time, he was intent on not letting that flame-burning mage get off another spell. Ammudien hastily drew the runes of his next spell before using his wand to throw them at the feet of his opponent.

The sand at the fire mage's feet turned to quicksand and began pulling the hooded figure down. The fire mage struggled against the constant suction but was losing the battle. It was soon apparent that the ground would swallow the fire mage if nothing changed. This forced the fire mage into an act of desperation.

He began quickly and crudely drawing some very different runes from those drawn before. Instead of fire red runes, the new runes were pale blue and wispy. The sinking mage swirled his wand around the runes until they formed a circle and swirled in synchronization with the wand. Next, the mage held the swirling runes over his head. A funnel of wind descended from the heavens directly over the fire mage. The tornado pulled against the suction of the quicksand to counter the gulping ground's effect.

Ammudien watched, completely confounded by what he was witnessing. The fire mage was also using wind magic, something very atypical for mages who traditionally focused on a single discipline. Additionally, the mage's wind magic appeared to be just as strong as the fire magic had been, as the controlled tornado slowly began to pull the mage from Ammudien's summoned quicksand.

Ammudien, still stunned by what he was seeing, just watched as the other mage was pulled free from his spell. The quicksand spell faded, the ground returned to a more normal state, and the mage released the conjured tornado, dropping him back to the solid ground again. Ammudien froze in fear, not sure what to do next against someone so unusual when it came to magical abilities.

The gnome's new nemesis did not share that fear.

Sensing Ammudien's hesitation, the fire mage dropped to a knee and began awkwardly writing new runes in the sand. This immediately caught Ammudien's attention and snapped the gnome out of his daze. The fire mage was now attempting to perform terra magic as well.

Unsure of what else to do, Ammudien decided to go with reckless abandonment. The gnome chose not to cast another spell but rather to run towards his opponent. Ammudien's tiny little legs shuffled as fast as they could to move the gnome over the sand and in the direction of the distracted mage.

The terra magic seemed to be less familiar to the fire mage. The mage made some mistakes with the runes that caused his first attempt to cast the spell to fail, then another mistake that forced the mage to cancel the spell and start a third time. Through the entire series of attempts, the fire mage was so focused on trying to cast the unfamiliar spell that the approaching gnome went completely unnoticed. Ammudien jumped at his foe. Leading with his feet, he kicked the mysterious mage in the chest, disrupted the mage's spell, and knocked the unusual mage backward to the ground.

The two mages both hit the ground. Ammudien was the first to get up. It was time for round two of the dueling mages.

***

The armored soldier readied his sword and set his feet. It was not a good strategy to rush into a fight while outnumbered three to one against enemies with unknown skills and abilities. The better plan was to make them come into his defended position.

Riorik, Nordahs, and Wuffred all drew their swords once they reached the flat sands at the base of the dune.

Nordahs instinctively reached for his bow first but quickly realized that his bow would be of little use against someone covered in armor from head to toe. The experienced archer immediately recognized that there were few points of weakness that his bow could exploit, so he opted for his sword instead.

Riorik immediately noticed something extremely worrying about his unknown foe. The sword the stranger held and the breastplate he wore were both made of a green ore that looked very similar to the shield and leggings they had found previously.

"I guess this was our competition," Riorik thought to himself.

"Careful friends, he looks to wield the sword and breastplate we sought. This will not be an easy fight," Riorik whispered to his friends in a hush tone, hoping not to alert his new enemy to their knowledge.

His attempts were in vain.

"Ahh, so you know what it is that I bear?" the masked soldier asked, obviously hearing the young elf's low-toned warning.

"Then you know that there will be no victory other than mine," the unknown fighter added.

The three young rangers shared a look of concern and worry among themselves.

"We can still do this," Riorik assured the others.

The armored individual just laughed at Riorik's words.

"Together?" Nordahs asked.

Riorik and Wuffred nodded in agreement.

The three novice Rangers charged their opponent. It was the attack the armored one had anticipated. A small chuckle could be heard from behind the mask as the friends rushed their target.

The initial flurry of attacks was quick but ineffective. Riorik and Nordahs were able to sprint ahead of Wuffred so when they attacked it was only two against one. Their foe showed his skill immediately as he easily dodged Riorik's strike with a simple side-step before casually deflecting Nordahs's blow with the flat of his own sword. The side-step sent Riorik stumbling past his target before falling face first into the sand, while Nordahs's deflected attack spun the young elf away and towards the water. This meant that Wuffred was alone in his assault.

The young human lowered his sword, held it tight to his side, and charged straight at his opponent. Wuffred wanted to impale his enemy on the end of his blade. This attack, like those of his friends, failed miserably. The armored individual just waited until the last second of Wuffred's charge before spinning away from the blade. And as he spun, the masked foe used the pommel of his sword to smack Wuffred in the back of the head, sending the human Ranger rolling forward onto the sandy ground.

The three Rangers regrouped and looked at their fearsome foe again. Their opponent stood calm and still. Their attacks had done nothing except embarrass themselves. Wuffred's head throbbed from where he had been struck with the butt of the sword, and he was now breathing heavily. Riorik and Nordahs recognized this as the early warning signs of their friend's anger beginning to rise. This frightened them to an extent, but at the same time filled them with glee at what it could mean for their new enemy.

"Remember, Wuffred, he is the enemy, not us," Riorik casually reminded his berserker friend.

"Yeah, well, I can't make any promises, you know that," Wuffred emotionlessly responded.

The armored individual opposite of them heard their words but did not comprehend their meaning.

Aware that they could be heard, the three did not speak about their tactics. They knew they needed to surprise their enemy, so instead they just exchanged a series of looks and head motions to convey their next attack plan with one another. Within seconds, the plan was set without a single word spoken.

Nordahs went first.

The elf ran towards his target. Then, at the last minute, the elf sprang high up into the air and struck down with his sword at his foe's helm.

The attack was defended.

The armored person watched as the young, nimble elf jumped high above his head but was quick to raise the green sword for a proper defense against such an attack.

The three friends had counted on this move by their opponent. It looked as though their plan had succeeded.

Wuffred had taken off running right after Nordahs, so as their opponent watched the flying elf, the human was readying his attack aimed at the torso. As the mysterious fighter moved to defend against Nordahs's aerial attack, Wuffred lowered his shoulder and rammed the unsuspecting target right in the chest. Wuffred's charge was strong enough to lift the armored soldier from his feet and knock him to the ground with a heavy thud.

Next was Riorik.

Riorik had taken off running behind Wuffred. Like Nordahs, Riorik leapt into the air, soaring over Wuffred. He dropped from the air with his sword pointed directly down towards the ground and right at his target. He hoped the momentum from his jump and his weight behind the sword would drive his blade through his foe's armor.

The downed fighter was stunned by Wuffred's blow but was still alert enough to see Riorik's incoming attack. There was barely enough time to react but react the fighter did. Even under the weight of his armor, their fallen foe was able to roll to one side far enough to dodge Riorik's blade.

This move gave Riorik a clear look at the stranger's cloak hanging from the shoulders of his armor for the first time. As Riorik dropped from the air, the young elf spied something familiar, something that he had not seen for a long time.

The cloak was clasped together by a golden pin. A golden pin that looked exactly like the one Riorik had found in the forest outside of Rishdel before joining the Rangers Guild. This person wore the same gold pin that the old elf in the post office had said was once worn by Rangers. This confused Riorik to the point that he was so focused on the pin that he did not notice that his sword had stuck in the sand but missed his target. The elf just stood there holding his sword's handle, deep in thought about the pin's meaning.

His thoughts were soon interrupted as he felt a hard impact on his side. The fallen foe had spun around and kicked Riorik away from his sword before rolling back to his feet.

However, now standing, the armored individual found himself surrounded by the three Rangers.

The three friends exchanged another series of glances before their next attack. All three attacked at the same time now. Riorik attacked from one side and swung his sword high, at the stranger's head. Nordahs, from the opposite side, attacked low, swinging his sword at the stranger's belly. Wuffred, who was in front of the stranger, tried again to drive his sword through his opponent's chest.

The results were shocking to the trio.

Their enemy only blocked Riorik's attack. Again, the green sword came up to defend the blow, which turned Riorik to the side. This defensive move was followed by a hard punch to Riorik's jaw that sent the young elf spinning away. The other two attacks were allowed to hit their target.

Nordahs's sword hit the bottom of the green breastplate and stopped. There was absolutely no penetration. The young elf then sliced away with his sword to try and cut through the armor, but his blade only slid off the protective garment without leaving so much as a scratch on the surface.

Wuffred, charging from the front, lowered his sword to his side and held it perpendicular to his body. The berserker's goal was to ram his sword through his target at the ribs and impale their armored opponent.

His plan almost worked too.

The first two attacks from Riorik and Nordahs had successfully distracted the armor-clad stranger to the point that Wuffred's attack went undefended. Unfortunately, his opponent's armor proved to be too strong. The human ran at full speed with the tip of his sword pointed directly at his target, but as the blade struck exactly as where he had intended, the blade's tip snapped as if it were little more than a twig. The green armor was not penetrated, or even scratched for that matter, by either attack. It was immediately clear to Wuffred that the stories about the armor's mythical qualities were true beyond their illuminating glow.

Riorik was still stunned by the assault and did not see Wuffred's failed attack, but Nordahs had. Nordahs too recognized the armor's ability for what it was and quickly realized the seriousness of their current situation. Nordahs turned to his elven friend and quickly shouted for his attention.

"Riorik!" he shouted, trying to get his friend to snap out of the daze he suffered from the blow taken in combat.

Riorik shook the cobwebs from his head as he tried to silence the ringing in his ears. He had heard his friend's call and looked in Nordahs's direction.

"The pants!" Nordahs yelled. "Put on the pants!"

It took a stunned Riorik a few seconds to fully comprehend the words before tossing his backpack to the ground and pulling the flexible pants from its depths. He was still too in shock to question anything as he effortlessly pulled the pants over his leather boots and other pants. The green pants slid on as if nothing else was beneath them. Riorik released the top of the pants at his waistline and the entire garment quickly adjusted to his spindly frame to make for a perfect fit.

Meanwhile, Wuffred and his foe still stood toe to toe with only Wuffred's broken sword between them, still pressed against the unscathed armor. Wuffred watched in awe as Riorik donned the pants that they had only recently acquired. His foe, on the other hand, having seen similar astonishing capabilities in his own armor, immediately recognized Riorik's new apparel for what it was—another piece of the missing Ascension Armor.

The well-equipped foe threw a hard right-hook at an unsuspecting Wuffred's jaw. The powerful blow landed and sent the human in Ranger clothing flying away. It was clear that this person had an equal or greater strength than the barbarian Wuffred, despite being much smaller.

Free of Wuffred's presence, the unidentified person turned towards Riorik and began to walk towards his next prize.

Chapter 10

Riorik took his first step after putting on the legendary greaves, and he was immediately shocked by the sensation. His feet felt lighter, faster, and more responsive to his thoughts. He found himself moving about on the soft sand that covered the ground with a greater ease than he had before. It seemed the powers rumored to be bestowed by the armor onto its bearers were true. The greaves gave Riorik an improved agility. And their foe's incredible strength relative to his size was made possible, given that he obviously wore the breastplate.

It was now a fight of speed versus strength.

But, before that fight could unfold, the hard blow to Wuffred's jaw had awakened the berserker within. It would first be a fight of strength versus strength.

An enraged Wuffred approached his distracted enemy from behind. As the armored opponent walked towards Riorik, Wuffred wrapped his arms, now surging with berserker strength, around his target's abdomen. The berserker squeezed with all of his might. A lesser armor would have been crushed under the force, but the breastplate held strong.

Even with the breastplate's enhanced strength, the unknown foe struggled to free himself from Wuffred's grasp. With his free hand, the unseen enemy pulled in vain against Wuffred's interlocked hands in a failed attempt to break the hold. The only saving grace was that Wuffred had not trapped his arms with the move. This left the unnamed king free to awkwardly stab and slice at Wuffred's forearms with the green sword.

The wounds on Wuffred's arms opened wide and deep against the sharp blade's edge. Blood rushed from the open injuries, but the berserked Ranger never flinched. Pain was not something a berserker in a full blood rage would ever recognize. This filled the trapped fighter with a small sense of fear for the first time.

Riorik, filled with confidence thanks to his increased agility and Wuffred's current success, decided it was time to move in and finish this fight before his friends obtained any more injuries. With fleet feet, Riorik quickly covered the distance to his opponent. However, once there, he realized that he had moved so quickly that he had not adequately thought his attack through. His sword had no chance to penetrate the magic breastplate. His only targets were the head and legs of his enemy, but both were also heavily armored. Also, the young elf quickly realized that his enemy's sword arm was still free as it swung in his direction, forcing him to quickly side-step the attack and move out of range for any additional attacks.

Wuffred, who only got more enraged as his arms continued to bleed, decided squeezing was not the answer. Now, the incredibly strong berserker lifted his opponent from the ground and rested the armored foe on his shoulder, being sure to keep his enemy's sword away from his body. And even before his startled challenger could fully comprehend the current predicament, Wuffred dropped backward to the ground, driving his enemy's head and shoulders into the floor of the oasis.

Riorik watched in awe as the force of the impact drove the two fighters apart. Wuffred rolled away before standing up. His challenger was slower to recover but was obviously uninjured by the move. The only positive change for Wuffred was that the impact had made the masked fighter drop the legendary sword.

Riorik saw the sword laying in the sand and knew this to be his opportunity.

"I can sprint over there, grab the sword, and put an end to this fight once and for all," Riorik thought to himself.

Using his newfound agility and speed, Riorik raced towards the loose weapon. Unfortunately for Riorik, the downed opponent was still close enough to his prized possession to pick up the blade before the nimble elf could. Once more, an unprepared Riorik was forced to retreat. The elf was relying too much on his new speed and not thinking beyond that overwhelming excitement stemming from the armor's gift to plan on what to do if his speed failed or what to do next if his speedy plan succeeded. Riorik was not being the thoughtful and prepared leader that had brought his group this far in their quest, and it was leaving the elf, and his friends, vulnerable.

Meanwhile, Nordahs circled the ongoing fight in a defensive posture, keeping a close eye on his friends. Nordahs had recognized that his rusty blade would only shatter against the power of the breastplate and that his arrows would only be dulled against the massive armor that covered his target from head to toe. Realizing that any attacks from his weapons were futile, Nordahs opted to observe and offer suggestions to his better equipped friends when he saw the opportunity. So far, few opportunities presented themselves against such a powerful foe, leaving Nordahs with little to do but watch.

Once more, the armored enemy turned his attention to a nearby Riorik. He was intent to get the greaves that now covered the young elf's legs. So much so that he forgot about the approaching berserker.

As Wuffred approached his target from behind, the angry berserker let out a very loud yell. The deafening yell caught the attention of the group's armored enemy, who spun around to face its source.

It was a decision that he soon came to regret.

As the armor-clad foe turned to look in Wuffred's direction, the crazed berserker threw a powerful overhand right punch. The berserker's large, bloody fist landed just above his target's left eye. The blow was so strong that it curled the edge of the non-magical helm just above the armored king's eye to the point that the armor actually cut into his skin. Blood began to immediately gush from the wound and ran into the now injured king's eye, partially blinding him to what came next.

Wuffred followed up his first attack with another punch. This time it was a left uppercut to his staggered enemy's chin. It was another super powerful blow from the Ranger, filled with the blood rage of his hybrid heritage. This time, the blow lifted his opponent, heavy armor and all, off the ground and sent him flying backward several feet. In addition, the impact was so hard that it dislodged the helm that rested on Wuffred's enemy's head and sent it flying off to the side, revealing their enemy's face for the first time.

***

Meanwhile, Ammudien had been careful to keep his distance from the brawl below as he continued his fight against the unknown mage. The two mages had continued trying to assault each other with various spells, but most of the time, they only ended up countering one another. Ammudien would cast an entrapment spell only to have the other mage escape. The robed mage would sling fireballs at the gnome only to have them blocked by rocks or sand walls summoned by the tiny terra mage. Despite the difference in their robes, the two mages appeared to be evenly matched.

Both mages could be seen glancing towards the oasis as their own fight wore on. They were both concerned about their allies fighting below. Ammudien's face was one of great concern after seeing the repeated failed attempts to attack the green armor, but a smile did come eventually, along with a faint sense of hope, after seeing Wuffred finally go berserk.

"No matter how strong that armor is, it does not stand a chance against him now," the gnome thought to himself once he realized that Wuffred's rage was finally released.

But it was in this moment of distraction that Ammudien almost met his own end.

As Ammudien watched with glee as Wuffred gripped the armored foe in a reverse bear hug, the robed mage took advantage of the gnome's attention being placed elsewhere. The unknown fire mage quickly went back to the basics, the spells easiest to cast, and quickly scribbled out a fireball spell that was sent hurdling towards Ammudien.

Luckily for Ammudien, the fireball's intense heat alerted the gnome to its growing presence. The short mage reacted as quickly as he could, jumping to the side to avoid the flaming projectile headed his way. The move was not a large one but was sufficient to get the gnome out of the fireball's direct path.

Unfortunately, however, that was about all the little move did for Ammudien. The fireball struck the ground just a few feet behind where the gnome had been standing and exploded, sending burning shards out in all directions. One of the burning pieces of shrapnel struck Ammudien's right hand, his wand holding hand. The searing pain caused him to drop his wand into the sand. The small wooden wand fell tip first and stuck up from the sand like a sprouting tree jutting up from its roots.

A panicked Ammudien quickly used the sleeve of his robe and his left hand to remove the magical burning shard from the back of his hand. And then, after he had a chance to calm down from the initial shock of the injury, Ammudien realized that he had dropped his wand. He wasted no time in looking for it, but as he spun around, the bottom of his robes flared out and covered what little bit of his wand that was protruding from the sand near his feet.

"Now's my chance," the robed mage thought as he watched Ammudien flailing about, trying to find his dropped wand.

Feeling confident that he had some time, the fire mage started carefully drawing a new set of runes in the air with his wand. These runes were very different from other runes the two mages had drawn throughout their prolonged battle. Where most runes shined with the color of the discipline used to learn the spell, these runes glowed a dark purple, a color not affiliated with any discipline taught at the Mage Academy in Mechii. Not only that but the runes appeared to be deteriorating as the hooded mage drew them, almost dripping from the air.

As he completed the ominous runes, the robed mage flicked his wand in Ammudien's direction. The ruins faded away as they turned into a dark purple bolt flying towards the gnome.

Ammudien, completely unaware of the new magic headed in his direction, decided that spinning around aimlessly was not working. Now, he dropped to his knees and began feeling about in the sand with his hands as he still searched for his missing wand. It did not take him long to find it, now that his robes were no longer obscuring his vision.

Ammudien quickly grabbed his wand and pulled it from the sand and looked up just as the purple bolt flew over his head and splashed against the sandy hillside behind him. Much like the fireball before, the purple bolt exploded on impact like a water balloon and sent drops of purple ooze flying through the air. Once more, Ammudien had dodged the direct attack, this time without even trying, but he was unable to avoid the debris.

A drop of the purple ooze landed on the heel of one of the gnome's silken boots. The soft, thin material immediately rotted away, exposing the gnome's skin on the back of his foot. Ammudien was both angered and perplexed by the attack. He had no knowledge of any spell that would cause such an unnatural effect. All the magic taught at the Mage Academy was rooted in nature's elements, like fire, water, wind, and ground. What happened to his boot was not part of those elements. The mysterious mage was using magic from some other discipline, most likely a banned discipline, and that made Ammudien very upset.

"Oh, so you can't win in a fair fight, is that it?" Ammudien called out, very angry that the other mage had resorted to what Ammudien could only assume was forbidden magic.

Ammudien instantly sprang to his feet and began scribbling some new runes of his own. His runes were an almost transparent blue, almost ghostly in appearance.

"If that's how you want it, try this on for size," the angry gnome shouted, as he swept his wand down through the runes, pushing them into the ground before flicking his wand back up to the air as if to raise the runes from under the sands. However, as he raised his wand to the sky, it was not the runes that rose from the ground but three ghostly spirits that surrounded the robed mage.

The three apparitions immediately began clawing and scratching at the panicked mage. Ammudien's opponent was unable to cast any spells at first, as he was too busy trying to defend himself from his otherworldly attackers. Their claw-like fingers tore at the unknown mage's robes, shredding one of his sleeves as he used his arm to block as much as he could while he tried desperately to scratch out some rough runes with his wand hand.

Eventually, the vapor-like runes were complete and the assaulted mage used his wand to fling the runes to the opposite side of the oasis. The runes flew with great speed towards the other side until they hit the sand dunes there. As the runes struck the sand, a flash of light exploded from the robed mage's position, evaporating Ammudien's summoned spirits.

When the light faded, Ammudien no longer saw the other mage. Where the mage had been standing was now empty. Ammudien looked across the oasis to where the runes had landed. Standing where the runes had struck was now the other mage. Immediately, Ammudien realized that the other mage had used a teleport spell to escape. Ammudien now sensed a weakness in his otherwise evenly matched opponent. All there was to do now was finish him off, but first, Ammudien would have to cross the oasis himself. But, unfortunately for Ammudien, the terra mage had not mastered teleportation yet, which meant he would have to cross the oasis on foot.

As the gnome made his way down the sandy hillside that had been his arena for the last several minutes, he watched with glee as Wuffred's berserk attack had knocked the heavily armored fighter to the ground for a second time but was still too far away to see his now exposed face. Recognizing that the armor welding fighter was stunned and vulnerable, Ammudien felt compelled to alert his friends to their opportunity.

"Now, Riorik, attack!" the gnome shouted at his elven friend.

***

Riorik, seeing the armored opponent on the ground and hearing Ammudien's call to attack, quickly sprang into action. The young elf began sprinting towards his downed target with an unparalleled speed. After what felt like just a few steps, Riorik was already within striking distance. With a simple push of his legs, Riorik jumped high into the air, higher than he had ever jumped before. The others watched in awe as he flew so high, yet so easily.

Riorik firmly grabbed his sword's handle and held it so the tip pointed down. He planned to drive the sword through his foe using the force and momentum of his fall to penetrate any defense put before him.

As he fell from high above his target, an echoed shout rang throughout the oasis.

"No!" was the yell that seemed to come from both sides of the oasis.

In fact, that was exactly what happened. Both mages had yelled out at the same time as they watched Riorik launch his attack, but both for very different reasons.

The robed mage on the opposite side of the oasis cried out in fear and desperation. He saw Riorik's attack as the fatal blow that would kill his king. Ammudien, on the other hand, yelled because he knew Riorik's choice of attack to be folly.

Riorik plummeted from above, posed to strike a powerful blow. But, just as Riorik approached the ground, inches before his blade found its target, his descent was interrupted. The elf felt a strange force pushing against him, deflecting his trajectory as if some unseen force was repelling his attack. And before Riorik could grasp what was happening, the falling elf was repelled away from his target. The unseen force had pushed the elf up and away from his downed opponent, but not before he had gotten a look at his foe's uncovered face.

Riorik flew backward completely befuddled. Not only was his attack thwarted by an invisible force, but their foe was another elf. Riorik did not recognize the face looking back up at him, but it was definitely the face of a wood elf like him and Nordahs. The high cheekbones, the pointed ears, piercing blue eyes, the silvery blonde hair—all the unmistakable characteristics of a wood elf. The fact that he was fighting an unknown wood elf was more surprising and confusing to Riorik than the unexplained force that repelled his attack.

"It must be some magic from that strange mage," Riorik thought to himself as he fell to the ground away from his intended target.

Relieved that he had been spared by what he could only assume was his mage ally's magic, the unmasked elf wasted no time in recovering. He scrambled back to his feet with his sword still in hand. With his other hand, the unknown elf scooped up his battered helm and placed it back over his bloodied face. His face had been exposed, something that had not happened in some time, but he was intent on not leaving it that way. Nordahs and the strange mage both tried to get a peek at his face, but he was too quick. Riorik was the only one to see his face this day.

With his face covered once more, the new elf once again turned his attention to Riorik. The younger elf was still staggered by the events before and was unprepared to defend himself. The older, more heavily armored elf knew this to be the perfect chance to strike and take his prize.

"Those pants will be mine!" the strange elf yelled at Riorik, as he marched across the sand towards the younger elf.

Nordahs contemplated rushing to his friend's aid but knew that he could do nothing to stop or even slow the more powerful elf's advance. Instead, Nordahs opted to stay out of the fight between those two and focus his attention on keeping the unknown elf's mage friend from interfering. The crafty elf sheathed his sword and swapped to his trusty bow. He quickly nocked an arrow and drew the bow's string to a full draw before leveling his arrow directly at the unfriendly mage still standing on the sandy hillside.

"If he starts to draw a rune, I will put this arrow right through his wand hand," Nordahs thought to himself, as he kept his sights and the bow's aim firmly on the mage.

The hooded mage did not move. He made no attempt to cast a single spell as he watched the fight below continue to unfold with extreme curiosity. After all, it appeared that his master was about to win and claim his next piece of the armor. That would give the unnamed and self-appointed elven king three pieces of the legendary armor and that would surely be enough for him to complete his conquest of Corsallis.

Opposite the opposing mage's opinion, Ammudien was horrified at what he saw. Riorik was on the ground and visibly shaken. The better equipped and more skilled fighter approached. Ammudien knew that the fight was not in Riorik's favor at this point. But, before despair overwhelmed the gnome, a thought popped into his head.

"Of course! Why did I not think of this sooner?" the gnome whispered to himself, somewhat ashamed that he had not thought of it sooner.

Ammudien dropped to the ground, pulled the shield from his pack, and laid it on the sand. He then began drawing runes in the sand like the runes he'd used in the temple under the watchtower to move the stone slab covering the sarcophagus. As soon as he was finished drawing the runes, he quickly flicked his wand in Riorik's direction. The runes created a cushion of sand under the shield and sent it flying towards the gnome's downed friend.

"Riorik, catch!" Ammudien shouted as the shield zipped towards the elf.

The armored elf walked around Riorik's legs and towards the young elf's head. He did not want to take a chance of damaging the greaves that he lusted over. As he stood over Riorik's face, the masked elf raised his sword with both hands and prepared to drive his sword through Riorik's chest, much like Riorik had intended to do with his failed attack before.

But, before the stronger elf could deal the fatal blow, Riorik snatched the flying shield out of the air and held it over his chest, directly under the other elf's sword. The standing elf drove his sword down with all his natural might, along with the extra might given to him from the breastplate that covered his chest. The sword plunged down towards Riorik with great force and speed but stopped in mid-air, just inches from the shield.

The sudden and unexpected stop of the sword caught the aggressor by surprise. He wanted to kill Riorik and would not be denied his prize. He pulled the sword back up before driving it down the second time. Again, the sword came to a sudden and abrupt halt, just inches from the shield. It was as if something was pushing the sword away from the shield, like how Riorik's greaves were repelled from the breastplate.

Convinced this was one of the mages' doing, he angrily growled to his mage.

"If you are doing this, then stop it! If this is not your doing, then it is his, and I command you to kill him. I will have my prize!" he yelled to his mage, obviously insinuating that one of the two mages were responsible for stopping his sword from finding its target.

"It was not me, my king," the raspy-voiced mage quickly replied, hoping to assure his master that he had not acted against him.

But, at the same time, the mage had not taken his eyes off Ammudien since teleporting away from the gnome's last attack. The robed mage knew that it was not the magic of his opponent either. Ammudien had not made a gesture indicative of spellcasting since sending the shield to Riorik's aid. The unknown mage was just as stumped as his master was regarding the force that was preventing him from killing the young elf at his feet.

Refusing to give up, the armored elf continued trying to spear his sword into Riorik's chest. With each attempt, the sword was stopped just before it reached the shield. So consumed by rage and desire, the unnamed king failed to notice that the shield in Riorik's hand was the last missing piece of the Ascension Armor of lore. All four pieces of armor were now all in the same place at the same time and locked in combat.

As Riorik's would-be killer stood above him and tried in vain to force the sword into Riorik's flesh, the light faded and Riorik was consumed by a shadow. It was the shadow of a still very enraged Wuffred leaping over the young Riorik and tackling the other elf.

The pair hit the ground with Wuffred firmly mounted atop his foe. The berserker let loose a flurry of punches. There was no real pattern in his punches as he just continuously and furiously threw punch after punch. Some punches missed completely, hitting the ground, and showering the area with sand ejected from the force of each blow. Others hit his opponent's helm, further distorting the armor's appearance and causing significant pain to its wearer as the metal pinched, crushed, and cut into his head with each strike from Wuffred's thunderous blows. And the rest landed against the Ascension Armor breastplate. These blows did nothing to the downed elf's armor, but inside the armor, the self-proclaimed king felt each impact as the concussive force from each blow rippled through his body. The armor would not break, but the armored elf was not so sure now that his bones could withstand much more of this assault. Undeterred, Wuffred continued to madly slam his bare fists against his foe as he threw more and more haymakers in his rage. And while the attacks did little to the magical armor protecting his opponent, they did manage to seriously injure Wuffred's hands, not that the berserking Ranger was in any condition to notice or care.

The battered elf grew angry under Wuffred's steady assault.

"*Get off of me*," the irate elf yelled as he managed to throw a left hook from his position.

Once more, the elf managed to strike Wuffred's jaw, only this time from the other side. The hit had the same effect as the previous one, sending Wuffred flying. This allowed the beaten and bloodied elf to get back on his feet again, something that did not bode well for the others previously. Unlike before, this time the armored elf kept his attention focused on Wuffred. The human in Ranger's clothing was unlike anything that he had encountered before, with his enormous strength and undeterred desired to fight. Finally, the elf realized that Wuffred was the obvious threat among the group and that if he wanted any chance at getting the armor away from Riorik, then he would have to kill Wuffred first.

The two charged at one another. The elf with his sword at the ready and Wuffred with his fists clenched in a berserker rage. As the two drew closer, the armored elf knew that he could not let himself get within reach of Wuffred's powerful grip again. He had managed to survive three attacks from the berserker, but just barely. With each encounter, the elf gained new scars that would tell the tale of his battle with the blood-raging human for years to come. He knew that he had been lucky to survive up to this point and that another close encounter with this strange human was likely to be his last. A new plan was needed, and the crafty elf quickly put one into action.

The armored elf slid to a stop in the sand and hoisted his sword up to his shoulder where he held it almost like a spear. Using the strength granted to him by the breastplate, the elf hurled the sword as hard and as fast as he could toward the rampaging berserker. Wuffred, in his berserker rage, made no attempt to deflect or block the sword flying towards him, a decision that would be his undoing.

The green blade buried itself into deep Wuffred's chest. The sword had cleaved the berserker's heart in two. The berserker blood that filled his veins was enough to propel him forward a few more steps, but without a beating heart to continue to feed his muscles with fresh blood, the berserker's body could go no more. Wuffred's muscles grew weak, causing him to stumble before collapsing to the ground.

As Wuffred's body fell to the ground, the berserker rage faded with the absence of flowing blood. The human Ranger quickly realized his fate. With his last breath, he uttered the only thought left in his mind.

"Asbin, please forgive me."

Riorik, Nordahs, and Ammudien cried out in unison at the sight of their friend's death. Unlike the others though, Riorik was not frozen in shock. No, the young elf felt an all-consuming rage of his own. With his sword in one hand and his new shield in the other, Riorik charged at Wuffred's killer. The elf screamed as he sprinted over the soft ground towards his new nemesis.

The other elf was quick to recover his sword from Wuffred's corpse, but thanks to Riorik's newfound speed, he barely had enough time to turn around and swing his sword with all his might in an effort to defend himself from his latest attacker. Between Riorik's increased speed and the other elf's enhanced might, the shield and sword got closer than they had before, to the point that the tip of the sword just contacted the edge of the shield.

In that instant, there was a bright flash emanating from the point of contact which was so bright that it could be seen by the guards atop the walls of Brennan and Tyleco. This was immediately followed by a shockwave that violently separated the two fighters. It sent Riorik flying in one direction and his opponent in the other. Not only that, but the shockwave was so powerful that it knocked Nordahs, Ammudien, and the other mage away as well. They all found themselves blown away from the oasis, and from each other.

Nordahs and Ammudien wasted no time in running to Riorik's landing point. And likewise, the other mage quickly made his way to where the force had thrown his master. The two groups were now separated by a fair distance, and both fighters were unconscious from their hard landings. The mage tried in vain to revive his master, while Ammudien only encouraged Nordahs to carry Riorik.

"We need to leave here. Now!" Ammudien pleaded with Nordahs.

"We have to kill that bastard for what he did to Wuffred!" Nordahs angrily replied.

"No, he has two pieces of the armor. Neither of us is any match for that power right now, and Riorik is likely seriously injured. We need to leave and regroup before we all end up like Wuffred," Ammudien said as he tried to reason with the conscious elf.

"What about Wuffred?" Nordahs asked. "We can't just leave him there. We have to go get him."

"There is nothing we can do for him, Nordahs. Wuffred is gone. It will only mean our deaths would join his if we returned now," Ammudien said, still trying to get through to his emotional friend.

"At least tell me what in the seven hells was that?" Nordahs asked as he waved his hands about in the air, referencing the shockwave that scattered the group.

"There will be time to discuss that later, but right now, I need you to pick up Riorik and run. I can't explain anything if we are dead."

The anger of Wuffred's death, the shock of getting thrown by an unseen force, and the annoyance of not getting any answers left Nordahs in a foul state but unable to argue with the gnome. Ammudien grabbed Riorik's sword and shield while Nordahs scooped up his friend and slung his limp body over his shoulder. With Riorik collected, the group moved as fast as Nordahs's feet could carry them and made their way back towards their campsite and away from the oasis, their opponents, and their friend's corpse.

Chapter 11

Captain Cooper had watched from his vantage point as the armored individual killed his suspect, Wuffred, by throwing a sword at him. Subsequently, Captain Cooper had also witnessed Riorik's emotional charge followed by the burst of light. The ensuing shockwave also reached the captain's position and knocked the city guard back down the sandy hill that he had watched from for the last several minutes.

The guard captain stumbled to his feet, and after regaining his bearing and balance, decided it best to leave. The power of the mages he witnessed was beyond anything he had seen before. He knew he would not be able to apprehend the mage who had attacked him previously. And, with Wuffred's death, he had no reason to continue pursuing Wuffred's friends. Not to mention that he was somewhat scared, after having been knocked down by an invisible force. There were things at play near that oasis that Captain Cooper wanted no part of now.

He easily made up his mind that he would make his way back home by following his steps back the way he came. This initially led him back to where Riorik and the others had made camp the night before. Still a little shaken up from the events at the oasis, Captain Cooper decided to stop at the campsite and catch his breath.

"What was that?" he asked himself as he tried to comprehend all that he had seen.

Captain Cooper continued to talk to himself. He wanted to rationalize what he observed but was not sure how.

"Was Wuffred a berserker? How else could he have such unbridled fury like that? That was stronger than my strongest guards combined. There's no other explanation for how he could toss someone in full armor like that. Such power!"

Being a human, Captain Cooper had heard the stories of the half-breed berserkers before, but he had never seen one before now. And, not even having any confirmation or previous knowledge about berserkers, Captain Cooper was certain that was the only reasonable explanation for what he saw Wuffred do. But, the city guard captain had a harder time rationalizing some of the other things he had witnessed.

"If Wuffred was a berserker, then how did that elf in that armor withstand such a brutal beating? Wuffred took him off his feet a few times and bashed him with some outrageously hard hits. I mean, I saw the elf's helmet go flying at one point, but the rest of his armor looked untouched through it all."

"And besides that, how in all of Corsallis was that elf able to hit back as hard as he did? Was that elf a berserker too? I've never heard of an elven berserker before, but I can't for the life of me find any other way to explain it. He went toe to toe with a berserker, and not only did he not die, but he managed to kill the berserker. That's just unheard of."

"And what about that other elf? He moved like lightning. I know elves are supposed to be agile and quick, but he was far quicker than anything I've ever heard of. Shoot, he was even quicker than the other two elves there. In the blink of an eye, he would go from here to there. And that jump, how did he jump so high? It had to be those mages using some of their sorcery. There's no other explanation for it. That had to be it."

The captain, like most people in Corsallis, had only ever heard tales of the Ascension Armor, and like everyone else, he believed them to be fairy tales and nothing more. At no point during the fight or in his thoughts afterward did it occur to him that he was witnessing all four pieces of the legendary armor in action or that the abilities of the armor were what gave Riorik and the other elf their elevated abilities. He sat there so enthralled by his thoughts that he did not notice the silhouettes coming over the hill and headed towards the camp.

***

"What was that? Why couldn't I kill that rotten elf who stole my pants? And what knocked me over here?" the armored elven king demanded to know from his mage ally once he had regained consciousness.

"I do not know, my Lord," was the reply from the raspy-voiced K. "All I know is that it was no magic of mine, and from what I could tell, nothing cast by their mage either."

"Then tell me, mage, how is it that my sword did not cleave that elf in two? I carry Raiken's sword that is said to be able to penetrate any armor, but I was unable to even scratch that puny Ranger want-to-be."

The king of Narsdin was very clearly aware of his sword's provenance. And the fact that he knew what the sword was capable of only increased his annoyance at having failed to kill Riorik when he had the chance. Now he wanted to know how he could have failed at killing such an easy target.

"I wish I knew, Sire, but I do not know for certain. The only thing that I can assume is that, because the one they called

Riorik bore Sagrim's Shield, the two counteracted one another, and that Raiken's sword cannot penetrate Sagrim's Shield."

This was the first time that Sagrim's Shield had been a thought in the armored elf's mind. He had been too consumed with thoughts of collecting the greaves from Riorik that he had not noticed Sagrim's Shield.

"What?" he yelled at the mention of Sagrim's Shield. "You mean to tell me that this Riorik elf had not one, but two pieces of the Ascension Armor, and we just let them escape with both?"

Desperate to calm his angered leader, the mage thought it important to put things in a different perspective.

"Well, I wouldn't say we let them escape. It was more of an unexpected event that forced us away from their presence. Had it not been for that unexplainable force, then surely you would have prevailed and gotten their pieces for yourself."

The mage's words did little to calm his master's anger.

"Worthless, that is what you are," the elf yelled at the mage. "I need answers and I need that armor, and you can give me neither. You knew the elf carried Sagrim's Shield, and you said nothing until now."

"He was given the shield after the fighting broke out. He used it to stop your sword, so I assumed you saw it too."

K's words stung the elf's ears. The mage unwittingly pointed out that he had the perfect opportunity to grab the shield as he stood over Riorik. If there was anyone to blame for Sagrim's Shield slipping through his fingers, it was him, and now he knew it. But, rather than admit his faults, the armored king elected to change the subject.

"Regardless, we must understand why Raiken's sword failed to pierce Sagrim's Shield and if there is anything else to learn about the armor," he declared.

"What would you have me do?" the mage asked of his master.

"Return to the Mechii. Your research there has been invaluable for our mission up to this point. Perhaps there is more for you to learn there before our next encounter," the mage's master answered.

"Yes, my Lord," the mage dutifully replied. "I will make haste in my return to Mechii. Any news I find will be promptly spirited to you via carrier as usual."

"That's a good boy," the armor-clad leader replied to the mage. "Now, hurry back to Mechii as you said. Do not dally here or anywhere in between. I look forward to your findings and your return to my side."

The mage nodded and bowed before his king. Then, the hooded figure calmly turned and began walking away in a southerly direction. The mage's head was filled with many of the same questions as was his master's, but he was less certain that Mechii would hold the answers to those questions. Regardless, the pessimistic mage slowly made his way towards Mechii as he was ordered.

***

"Ammudien, look there," Nordahs said as he pointed towards the campsite. "It looks like someone has decided to make our camp their own."

"Do you think it is one of those vile people from the oasis?" the gnome said as he squinted his eyes, trying to make out more details about their uninvited guest.

"No, this is someone different. They wear armor, so it's not the mage, but the armor looks different than the armor the other elf wore. In fact, this person looks distinctly human."

"Does he look like a threat?" Ammudien cautiously asked.

"It doesn't look like it," answered Nordahs. "But, considering what we just went through and the fact that we lost Wuffred and Riorik is still unconscious, I'd say it's probably best to proceed carefully. My vote is we nullify any possibility of a threat before it becomes real."

Eager to not lose another friend, Ammudien readily agreed with Nordahs's assessment and plan.

"I have just the thing," Ammudien announced, as he held out one of his little arms to stop Nordahs from continuing forward.

"Really? And what would that be?" asked Nordahs.

"Have you heard of a rock golem?" Ammudien asked rhetorically, with a sly grin on his face.

"Wait. You can summon rock golems? Why didn't you do that before Wuffred got murdered?" Nordahs asked back, rather angrily.

"Mainly because it takes a long time to cast that spell, which would have left me very vulnerable to the other mage. The key to using magic is to use it wisely. If I had attempted to use that spell back there, then Wuffred would not be the only friend you would have lost today."

"Then why not cast that spell before we rushed into battle to give us another ally in the fight? A powerful one, at that." the exasperated elf huffed.

Ammudien wasted no time in answering the question.

"The idea was to approach the oasis in a stealthy manner to launch a 'surprise attack'. Was it not?"

"Well, as you might have just noticed, there is nothing stealthy about a golem. They are big. They stand out. Their movements are not exactly silent. And as magical constructs, they do not understand the concept of stealth or sneaking."

"The golem's very presence would have given away our approach and ruined whatever advantage we may have held in that fight. Had our enemies been alerted to our presence sooner, the loss of life could have been worse."

Nordahs was still upset about his friend's death, but there was no mistaking the validity of Ammudien's logic. The gnome had successfully held off the other mage during the fight, which was apparently no small feat in itself, so if Ammudien said summoning rock golems would have been too risky, then Nordahs had little choice but to accept the gnome's assessment as the truth.

"Oh, all right then, I suppose," Nordahs somberly replied. "Then I guess let me see this rock golem now."

Ammudien easily recognized the sadness and disappointment in his friend's voice. The gnome turned to face his elven friend and patted his leg.

"I'm going to miss Wuffred too," Ammudien said to his friend. "I wish there had been something I could have done to have prevented that from happening, but I don't think there is anything any of us could have done to have prevented it."

The gnome tried to console his friend, but the mage's level of empathy and sense of loss was not as deep as the elf's, so his efforts, while kind, were not very effective.

"Yeah, I suppose you are right. So, what do you say, let's get this rock golem over there because Rio is really starting to get heavy," Nordahs replied.

Ammudien nodded in understanding that he had done little to cheer up his friend and that there were other matters that needed his attention right now. He dropped to the ground, made several piles of dirt of different sizes, and began slowly drawing runes around each pile. At first, the runes did not make a lot of sense to Nordahs as he watched the gnome's actions. Some piles had similar runes, while others were completely different.

After a minute of watching the mage, it dawned on the elf that the piles represented different parts of the golem's body. Some piles were for the legs, others the arms, one was the torso, and one was the head. The piles that had similar golden-brown runes surrounding them were apparently for the pairs of body parts, like the legs and arms, two sets of matching runes for two legs, and several sets of matching runes for fingers.

Eventually, the mage completed his drawings. But, unlike previous spells where he flicked the runes with his wand, this time the gnome mage walked to one of the piles of dirt, stuck the tip of his wand in the sand just beyond the edge of his runes, and proceeded to trace an outline around the piles of dirt and runes in the shape of a body. Once the outline was complete, it began to glow in the same golden-brown color as the runes. Ammudien took his wand and pushed it deeper into the sand and moved it towards the piles of dirt. As his wand moved, so did the outline. The gnome made the outline pass through the runes, pushing them forward into the piles of dirt they encircled until it touched the base of each pile. From there, Ammudien quickly pulled his wand from the ground. This set off a chain of events that caught a watching Nordahs completely by surprise.

As Ammudien pulled his wand from the ground, the outline pressed into the ground, creating a depression around the piles of dirt in the shape of the outline. Each pile began to compress, turning into large, solid stones starting at the bottom of the outline and steadily moving towards the top. It took only a few seconds for the transformation to be complete. When it was done, Ammudien and Nordahs stared down at the rocky form of a person, but the spell was still not complete.

Now, Ammudien moved to the rocky shape's head. He used his wand to draw two simple runes of the same golden-brown color on the lifeless golem's forehead. The runes hung over the stone head. With the runes complete, Ammudien used his wand to slowly push them into the stone before quickly stepping back away from his summoned companion.

A soft glow encompassed the golem as the rocky form began to slightly shake. Nordahs looked on with awe as the arms began to move up and down. Next, the legs began to bend and flex. The golem was slowly coming to life. Eventually, the golem used its arms to push its massive frame upright before its massive boulder-like legs lifted the enormous and heavy frame to a standing position. With the golem finally standing upright, the rocky minion turned and faced its master, Ammudien.

"Seize the intruder," Ammudien commanded his pet as he pointed to the lone person sitting in their campsite.

The golem made no sounds or gestures. It only turned away and began lumbering towards the campsite.

***

Captain Cooper had been so preoccupied with his own thoughts as he still struggled to come to terms with the fight he had witnessed at the oasis that he had no clue of the approaching threat. It was only when the golem got close enough to the camp to cast a shadow over his position that Captain Cooper realized he was no longer alone.

The Tyleco city guard captain sprang to his feet with a sense of urgency and quickly drew his sword from its scabbard. The alarmed human turned to face his unknown guest only to be shocked by what he saw.

It was not a person but a large walking pile of rocks. That was the last thing Captain Cooper expected to be confronted by, so the unusual sight caused him to pause briefly. But briefly was all the rock golem needed.

Ammudien's summoned minion reached out with its arms made of stone and used its rocky fingers to grab Captain Cooper's arms. For being made of rocks, the golem's grip was surprisingly gentle yet firm. At first, Captain Cooper struggled to free himself from his stony captor's grasp, but it did not take long for him to see the futility of continuing to attempt such an impossible task. Having surrendered to the reality of his situation, Captain Cooper looked around to find the golem's commander while locked in its iron-clad grip.

A minute later, the golem's master, Ammudien, confronted Captain Cooper. The trapped guard immediately recognized Ammudien and Nordahs as part of Wuffred's group from the oasis.

"I say," Captain Cooper said defiantly, "do you have any idea who I am? I am Captain Rory Cooper of Lord Veyron's city guard. I demand you order this thing to release me at once."

The captain was fully aware that if Ammudien wanted, the mage could have the golem rip him apart in an instant and that there was nothing the captive human could do to stop it. He only hoped that his authoritative tone and rank would inspire them to comply with his request.

Unfortunately for Captain Cooper, Ammudien was not moved by the human's words. Instead, Ammudien looked at his creation and twitched his head up without saying a single word. The golem, psychically linked to his creator, understood the command and hoisted Captain Cooper off the ground. The captain's feet dangled and kicked in the air as he began to fear the worst.

"We are far from Lord Veyron's reach," started Ammudien as he responded to the guard captain's order, "and I am in no mood to be annoyed by the empty threats and orders of a deserter right now."

The gnome's words struck the captain as odd. Ammudien had called him a deserter, obviously assuming that he had run away from his duties in the city guard. The notion that Captain

Cooper had deserted his post was insulting to the proud member of Tyleco's elite guard.

"I'm not a deserter!" he exclaimed, in retort to Ammudien's false assertion.

"Oh, really? Then how do you explain your singular presence here, so far away from Tyleco?" Ammudien asked as he continued his interrogation.

Meanwhile, Nordahs carried the still unconscious Riorik over to a nearby clearing before carefully laying his friend and ally on the ground. Riorik had been in this immobilized condition for several minutes already, and Nordahs began to worry more and more with each passing minute that his friend might never recover. But, the young elf knew that there was nothing else he could do but wait and hope that Riorik would wake up.

With Riorik sat down, Nordahs returned to Ammudien to help question the captive guard.

"So, what's the story with this fellow?" Nordahs asked as he walked back to his mage friend.

"Hmph," Ammudien huffed at the question. "He says that he followed us and Wuffred from the city, after seeing Wuffred and Asbin parting ways outside the city gate. He claims that he thought it was odd that Wuffred was in the company of a dwarf, since Wuffred supposedly told him that he was traveling with his mother and sister, so he assumed Wuffred was either a thief or a swindler. Personally, I think he just abandoned his post and is just another deserter."

Nordahs quietly disagreed with Ammudien's obvious disdain for deserters. After all, he, Riorik, and Wuffred were technically all deserters from the Rangers, but he did not think of himself or his friends as bad people for that. The guild elders had given him and Riorik an order that directly conflicted with the guild's purpose of protecting the people of Rishdel, Wuffred included, and conflicted with their own personal morals against killing an innocent person. To them, it would have been eviler for them to have remained in the guild than it was for them to become deserters.

"I don't know about you, Ammudien, but given that he did obviously see Wuffred and Asbin, it might stand to reason that there is some truth to his words. I'm not saying that he isn't a deserter of the city guard, but even if he is, that doesn't make him a bad person or a threat to us now."

The elf then turned his gaze to the captive human still dangling in the air, locked in the golem's grasp. Nordahs motioned for the captain to release his sword, which he did so without argument. Nordahs took the captain's finely crafted sword and slid it between his belt and his pants, allowing the blade to come to rest as the sword's guard held it in place.

"You're not a threat to us, right?" he asked rhetorically.

"No, I'm certainly not a threat, as you can see," Captain Cooper nervously replied.

"See? He's not a threat," Nordahs said as he looked back at the mage. "I think we can let him down now. Don't you?"

With the captain disarmed, Ammudien silently instructed his golem to put the human back down on the ground and to release him. The golem obeyed, and Captain Cooper felt the ground's firmness beneath his feet once more.

Chapter 12

Eventually, the unconscious Riorik began groaning as he started to regain consciousness and move about. The young elf shook his head from side to side, sending his long flowing hair swirling around his head and pointed ears. It had been several minutes since his fight with the armored elf ended with a bang.

"Umm, what happened?" Riorik asked, obviously still weary from his fight and its aftermath.

The commotion caught the attention of his friends and Captain Cooper, all of whom rushed to his side.

"I wish I knew what to tell you," Nordahs answered before anyone else. "One minute you were fighting and then there was a big flash. We were all blown away from the oasis, and when we found you laying in the sand, you were motionless. At first, I thought you were dead."

"Well, that's not the full story," Ammudien started, before being interrupted by a still groggy Riorik.

"And Wuffred? Where's Wuffred?" he asked, very concerned for his friend.

The gnome considered changing the subject away from their fallen friend but knew deep down that Riorik would continue to ask until they were forced to tell him. Ammudien knew that it would have to be said eventually, so he quickly decided it was best to deal with it now.

"He didn't make it, Rio," the mage calmly told his friend as he placed a reassuring hand on the elf's shoulder.

Riorik just stared back at Ammudien, who was face to face with the sitting elf, as he tried to process Wuffred's demise.

"No. No, that can't be," Riorik finally replied as tears ran down his cheeks.

Riorik knew the truth of the situation. He had seen Wuffred's death for himself but refused to accept it. Ammudien's confirmation of Wuffred's end meant the last of Riorik's hope for his friend was extinguished. It made the young elf very sad. He hung his head as he thought about his lost friend.

"Where is his body?" Riorik calmly asked, even though he knew the answer already.

"Back at the oasis," Nordahs answered as he squatted down to his friend's level.

"We had no choice," Nordahs continued, now that he could look Riorik in the face. "The force knocked us all away. If we went back for Wuffred's body, that would have left you there and vulnerable. I had to choose between mourning one friend or two. I chose to only mourn one."

"We have to go back for him," Riorik demanded as he looked back into his friend's eyes.

"Riorik, it's not safe, and you know that," Ammudien countered.

"I will not let that traitorous wood elf desecrate our friend's body!" Riorik exclaimed.

His words struck the others by surprise.

"What wood elf?" Nordahs asked curiously.

"The wood elf in the armor," Riorik instantly replied. "What other wood elf would I be talking about?"

"The person in the armor was a wood elf?" asked Ammudien, obviously unaware of what Riorik had seen in the battle.

"Yes, but not one I recognized," Riorik answered as he struggled to pull himself to a standing position.

Nordahs quickly jumped up to help his friend, remaining at his side to provide additional support while Ammudien continued to question Riorik.

"Are you certain it was a wood elf?" the mage asked next.

"I think I know a wood elf when I see one, especially seeing how I am one," Riorik hastily retorted at Ammudien's insinuation that Riorik misidentified the other individual.

"Okay. Okay. It was a wood elf," Ammudien decided capitulation was the best course of action at this point, rather than continue to doubt and infuriate his battle-weary friend. "But, since you didn't recognize him, can you describe him in case someone else here can?"

"Well," Riorik started, as he looked up and around at the campsite for the first time since regaining consciousness.

The young elf stopped suddenly at the sight of an unfamiliar face, Captain Cooper.

"Who is this?" Riorik slowly asked, obviously very cautious and apprehensive about the unknown addition.

"This is Captain Rory Cooper of Lord Veyron's city guard in Tyleco," Nordahs said, as he introduced the recently subdued human to his recovering friend.

"Captain Cooper witnessed our fight at the oasis after following Wuffred, and us, here from Tyleco," Ammudien explained.

Captain Cooper took the opportunity following Ammudien's brief introduction to offer his own reassurances and support to Riorik, just as he had the others while the elf was still unconscious.

"Believe me when I say that I mean no harm to your group. I only followed your friend
who led me here when I thought him to be a thief, but I see that my assumptions were wrong."

"I offer my condolences for your loss and just prior to your recovery offered to help
bolster support from Tyleco to help fight this unknown wood elf foe and his wizard."

"Wizard?" Riorik asked, confused by the terminology the guard captain used.

Magic bearers were generally considered mages or elementalists. The young elf had never heard the term 'wizard' used in connection to any modern magic welder. Wizards were the villains of a bygone era, who used magic for nefarious and often evil purposes. A wizard's ability to weld multiple forms of magic was one of the reasons why the Mage Academy now only taught mages a single school of magic. It was forbidden within the academy for a student to study any element beyond the one chosen at the time of acceptance into the academy. Modern wizards were unheard of and would be hunted down if found out.

"Yes, that was no mere mage I faced off against at the oasis," Ammudien answered. "Whoever that was, he knew at least three different schools of magic and did things that would be considered forbidden and illegal by the academy. There is no word to describe that kind of corrupted use of magic but wizard."

Riorik just looked at Ammudien and Nordahs before staring once more at the new human.

"And you're sure he's not part of that other group?" he asked his friends.

"Not entirely," Nordahs answered. "But, he did know an awful lot about Wuffred's visits to Tyleco, so we're fairly confident that he at least came from Tyleco."

"And," Ammudien chimed, "his presence would explain the odd findings my magic detected about someone or something following us since leaving the city."

Ammudien's words caught Captain Cooper by surprise.

"Wait! You mean to tell me that you knew I was following you the whole time?" the surprised guard captain asked of the mage.

"You could say that, yes," the gnome replied. "My magic detected the presence of something that seemed to be following us, but we were unable to identify the exact nature of what was detected. You kept yourself a good distance behind us, to the point that we did not feel threatened by what I felt, so we opted not to investigate it and continue pushing onward. So, yes, we knew something, or someone, was there but we did not know that it was specifically you."

"Wow!" Captain Cooper exclaimed at the mage's admission. "You know, that would be a very useful skill for the City Guard to have. It could come in very handy for our men, being able to detect threats outside the wall."

The intelligent gnome read between the lines of the captain's words and was quick to strike down that line of conversation.

"I'm sure it would be," Ammudien started. "But, that magic is reserved only for the mages of the Terra school at the Mage Academy and can only be used by those who are magically inclined. For a magician to teach that spell outside of the academy, or to anyone unaffiliated with the academy, would be illegal, resulting in both parties being marked as wizards, and subject to arrest by the academy."

Captain Cooper nodded in acceptance and understanding of Ammudien's answer but opened his mouth to say more.

However, before Rory could speak, Nordahs interjected in an attempt to get the conversation back on topic.

"While I know Ammudien's magic is impressive, I think that there are more pertinent things to be discussed, like the wood elf Rio saw at the oasis. Knowledge about who our unknown adversary is may prove more useful than a philosophical discussion about how to detect possible adversaries in the future."

His scathing words and firm tone made it obvious to the other two that their conversation would have to wait. They quickly agreed with Nordahs and turned their attention back to Riorik.

"So, what can you tell us about this unknown wood elf you saw?" Nordahs asked.

"I only saw his face for a second. After Wuffred knocked him to the ground and his helmet came off. It was when I jumped to attack him that I saw a brief glimpse before getting bounced away. Something I still don't understand either."

Ammudien piped up and interrupted at this point.

"I can explain that in a minute," the gnome offered, before allowing Riorik to continue.

"He looked like your typical wood elf," Riorik said as he started recalling the encounter. "His hair was a similar color to Nordahs and mine. His eyes were a soft blue. There were no distinguishing scars, marks, or tattoos on his face. About the only difference was that his face seemed a bit fuller than most wood elves and his jaw was squarer. It was obvious that he was a very robust elf."

"Do you think it's possible that it was a half-elf?" Nordahs asked.

"I would find that doubtful," answered Riorik. "Too many features were typically elven. I didn't see anything human about him. Same ears as us, same color hair, same eyes, same lips, everything. He looked distinctly elven, and wood elf at that, but not like anybody I would recognize from Rishdel."

Ammudien was the first to pick up on the obvious and put his theory out there for the group.

"Do you think it could have been your father?" the rational mage posited.

That thought had not crossed the mind of the two elves yet, and Ammudien's question quickly grabbed their attention. The gnome could see the thoughts and questions that raced through their minds through their eyes, as they both stared at Ammudien with their mouths agape.

With the two elves obviously dumbfounded by his suggestion, Ammudien decided to talk them through his theory.

"Think about it," he started. "Riorik's father is a wood elf who went missing from Rishdel many years ago after claiming to have found a missing piece of the Ascension Armor. Today, we fought an unknown wood elf who wielded half of the Ascension Armor set. Riorik's father said he found the armor, and this elf had the only pieces we haven't collected yet. Riorik's father disappeared before Riorik was born, so Riorik wouldn't recognize his father now. It all makes sense. The elf you fought against today, the elf that killed Wuffred, is your father, the same elf who killed Nordahs's father before disappearing. You wouldn't have recognized him, and he wouldn't have recognized you."

Ammudien's theory was intriguing and made sense as the others thought about it. Cyrel Leafwalker, Riorik's father, was often described as a larger-than-life elf who fought with the strength and ferocity of several elves. Even the sword he carried was bigger than the swords most elves carried, so obviously he was a strong elf. He did ramble in the days before his disappearance about finding something in the forest, and Riorik's group did find a ruin in the forest that looked to have held one of the missing armor pieces, but it had been looted before their arrival. The evidence was beginning to stack up, and everything did point to the mysterious elf being Riorik's missing father, Cyrel Leafwalker.

It was a thought that left Riorik feeling some very mixed emotions. He was partly excited about the fact that he might be able to find his father but was rather worried about the fact that his father had almost killed him. Then, there was the persistent sadness and rage surrounding Wuffred's death. But more than that, there was a concern for Nordahs. Riorik worried about his friend and how he felt about possibly confronting the elf who supposedly killed his father, all those years ago.

Would it be a reunion for Riorik and closure for Nordahs or would it be something worse? There was no way for the young elves to know until such time as they could find Cyrel again and talk instead of fight with him.

***

After a few minutes of silent contemplation regarding Ammudien's sound theory of the armored elf's identity, Riorik suddenly remembered the gnome's offer to explain the unusual events that prevented the two elves from killing one another.

"So, Ammudien," Riorik said, as he addressed his gnome friend, "you said you could tell me what happened during the fight that thankfully kept me and my father from killing one another. Is that true? Can you explain what happened?"

Ammudien just looked a Riorik and chuckled.

"You two really don't know much about the armor, do you?" he asked rhetorically.

"I mean, I know it was created from ore not of this land, that it glows blue, and that it was said to be lost generations ago, but other than that, no, not really," Riorik casually answered.

Ammudien just stared at Riorik after the elf's nonchalant response in the face of such obvious ignorance. The gnome's face twitched and contorted as he held back his contempt for Riorik's attitude while trying to find the best way to educate his friend without losing his temper. Eventually, the mage settled on an approach that might highlight the true power of the armor to the elf who now was in possession of two of the four pieces of legendary equipment.

"So, let's start with this," Ammudien began. "How do those greaves fit you?"

Riorik looked down at his green-shaded metallic pants before answering.

"Very nice," he said. "They are nice and snug, almost as if they were made for me."

"And you don't find that odd?" Ammudien asked, as he continued questioning the elf's powers of observation.

"Not really. They were made for a wood elf, and I am a wood elf, so it's kind of natural that they would fit me. Right?"

Ammudien hung his head and shook his head in disbelief.

"So, let me get this straight," the gnome started. "Pants that were smithed eons ago for a long-dead elf just happen to fit you perfectly today. And that in all the generations that have come and gone since those greaves were created, you, of all elves, are a perfect fit. It is a miraculous coincidence that you wear them and not another elf, like Nordahs, who is slightly of a different size to you, because no other elf could wear them so perfectly. Is that right?"

"Well, I mean, I haven't really thought about it," Riorik said. "I just put them on, and they fit. I just figured it was a wood elf thing."

Riorik's answer frustrated the gnome. Ammudien knew that logically Riorik's answer was ill-conceived and not fully thought out, but to an uneducated mind like Riorik's, the racial connection made sense. This meant that Ammudien would need to try a different tactic to make his point before continuing with his explanation.

"And the Shield of Sagrim?" Ammudien asked.

"What of it?" a confused Riorik replied questioningly.

"Do you not think a shield crafted for a gnome would be smaller than what you now hold?" Ammudien asked.

Riorik immediately grabbed the shield and held it up for inspection. The shield did seem to be of similar size to the shields some Rangers carried. Riorik tried to imagine Ammudien carrying a shield of comparable size, but he struggled to see how Ammudien, or any other gnome for that matter, would have been able to adequately use a shield of that size.

"Now that you mention it," Riorik started, as he lowered the shield once more, "it does seem a bit big for someone your size."

Ammudien casually strolled towards Riorik and the shield. The gnome calmly extended his arms and picked up the shield. As soon as Ammudien slid his arm into the grips behind the shield, the oversized shield shrunk to a more manageable size. It was now a shield capable of being used effectively by someone Ammudien's size. The gnome held the shield aloft to show it to Riorik and the others for a moment before tossing it back to Riorik. As Riorik caught the shield, he slid his arm into the shield's grips, and as it did with Ammudien, the shield automatically scaled its size to better fit and protect its bearer. Riorik, Nordahs, and Captain Cooper just silently stared at the shield in utter amazement.

"The mages who enchanted the armor all those years ago predicted that over time those who bore the armor would change size and shape. Warriors who became leaders were known to get rather portly with their new position of leadership, and the armor was intended to be passed down from generation to generation. With that said, the armor was imbued with the ability to automatically adapt to whoever possessed it. Those greaves would fit Nordahs, and even me for that matter, the same way they fit you, if one of us had put them on instead. That is also how your father was able to don the breastplate created for a dwarf. He possessed the breastplate, so it adapted to his body, his size."

It took a few seconds for Ammudien's explanation to sink in and be fully understood by the others. As it turned out, not only was the armor incredibly resilient and seemingly impervious to traditional weapons, but each piece granted its bearer with a gift like strength or agility and each piece would scale in size to best fit whoever possessed it. The legends and myths that surrounded the Ascension Armor were turning out to be more fact than anything else.

But, none of this explained what happened to Riorik during the fight.

"That's absolutely amazing," Captain Cooper said, breaking the silence that followed Ammudien's explanation.

"True," added Riorik, "but it does little to tell me why my attack failed the way it did."

"I was coming to that," replied Ammudien, "but first I wanted you to understand that there is more to the armor than just its resilience and its glow."

Ammudien paused for a moment to collect his thoughts before continuing.

"How can I put this so that you will understand what happened?" Ammudien mused aloud.

"The same mages and smiths who created this armor way back when foresaw the armor's potential for conquest and death. As such, they took measures to ensure that anyone looking to take the armor's full power for themselves would find it difficult."

"Consider this, the breastplate grants its bearer with tremendous strength and the greaves grant supreme agility. What would someone intent on conquest be capable of if they possessed the breastplate and the greaves? That speed and power would be almost unstoppable. As such, the armor was enchanted in such a way that those two pieces repel one another, so that one person could never wield both pieces at the same time. If someone was wearing the breastplate and then put on the greaves, the greaves would repel the breastplate from the wearer. Subsequently, if someone wearing the greaves tried to put on the breastplate, the breastplate would force the greaves from the wearer. You can have strength or speed but never both at the same time."

"Simultaneously, the sword and shield behave similarly toward each other. If someone tried to carry both, the two would repel one another in such a way that it would keep your arms spread apart and you would be unable to bring them together to mount an offense or defense of any kind. If you try to wield them both at the same time they will render one another completely useless while leaving you totally open and vulnerable to an attack."

"So," began Riorik, "by what you're saying, I wouldn't be able to wear the breastplate and greaves at the same time. Okay, I get that. But, that still doesn't explain to me what happened when I attacked him and vice versa."

"True, I did not explain that part yet," Ammudien conceded.

"It works along the same lines. The power of the armor was meant to bring peace, by more or less putting the four major races of Corsallis on equal footing, and to also ensure that peace by giving those same races sufficient power to quell any threat to the peace of Corsallis if they worked together."

Ammudien paused for a quick breath here.

"However, once again, those who came before us saw the potential the armor held to incite conflict among those who lusted for the power held by other armor bearers. So, similarly to how the armor repels itself from a single bearer, the armor actively works to keep separate bearers of the armor from clashing in combat using the armor. If two people have a disagreement, they cannot settle it while wearing the armor. The armor will repel the corresponding piece in combat too. Riorik, you jumped to attack a downed opponent. Your greaves and his breastplate repelled one another in that attack, and that force deflected you to prevent the pieces encountering one another. Likewise, when he tried to attack you, the shield repelled the sword so that no matter how hard he swung or how much force he pushed down with, the sword and shield refused to touch. And it was that same effect that blasted everyone apart in that final attack. Your speed from the greaves and his strength from the breastplate caused the armor to get so close to each other that the reaction was practically explosive in nature."

This revelation left the others speechless once more, as they processed the information given by the knowledgeable gnome.

Ammudien did not wait for their facial expressions to change before going on.

"It's all about balance. The breastplate is about raw power, which is balanced by the greaves and its incredible speed and agility. The sword is pure offense, while the shield is the final word in defense. In times of great danger, someone could bear either the breastplate or the greaves, and either the sword or the shield, while someone else could wield the rest. One versus one versus one versus one, or two versus two, but never three versus one—balance. It was meant to inspire cooperation but instead cultivated fear and paranoia that drove the races apart, instead of to a greater sense of togetherness."

"And now it seems that this elf's father," Captain Cooper said, as he pointed to Riorik, "looks to use the armor's power to tear down the walls of recluse created by each race in an effort to conquer us all."

"We don't know that!" Riorik quickly exclaimed, as he jumped to the defense of his assumed father.

"Orcs, gnolls, bandits, and a barbarian," Nordahs replied, without saying another word.

The others looked at him with confused and lost expressions, unsure of the meaning behind his words.

"These are the ones he has aligned himself with in his search for the armor. We have encountered them multiple times since leaving Rishdel, and every time, it was not a friendly meeting. I would have to concur with Rory's assessment that his intent is not one of benevolence."

Riorik glanced from face to face, looking at his friends. He could not argue with the experiences they all had shared, and there was nothing benevolent to be found in those encounters. He wanted to believe that his father could be found and the pair would return to Rishdel as a happy family, but he was now confronted with the reality of a father he did not know, a father who did not know him, and someone who seemed more interested in the armor Riorik carried than the fact that he was another elf. It caused the young elf to begin to question if his father had truly become lost to the armor and the madness that once protected it.

***

"So, it stands to reason that your father does not know the limitations of the armor," Captain Cooper suggested to the group.

"What makes you say that?" asked Ammudien.

"Well, if he is hunting the armor, despite already owning the breastplate and the sword, then that would suggest he thinks he can wield them all together," Rory answered.

"Perhaps, or maybe he is hunting for them to keep them from being used by those who may oppose him," Ammudien countered.

"He doesn't have to use them himself, but there is nothing that says he can't give them to his soldiers to make them stronger or that he couldn't just lock them away to keep them from falling into the hands of his enemy," the intelligent gnome added.

It annoyed Captain Cooper that he had not seen that strategic angle on his own. He was the guard captain in charge of Tyleco's security, so thinking of these types of plans and strategies were part of his everyday life. The fact that he was so enamored with the armor's power that he forgot his training and reacted so hastily was a huge personal disappointment. Nonetheless, he was quick to give proper credit where it was due.

"You have a great mind for critical thinking, my small friend. You could be a skilled military advisor, should you ever be so inclined," he told Ammudien in all sincerity.

Ammudien gave a simple nod and bow to the grand compliment bestowed upon him.

But, before Ammudien could respond further, Captain Cooper had more to say.

"But, if your assessment is correct, then we should ensure that he does not get his hands on this armor," Captain Cooper said, as he motioned to the armor held by Riorik.

"As such, I suggest that I take the shield and return to Tyleco. The shield will be safe there. I can talk with Lord Veyron about the imminent threat, and besides, the shield belongs to Tyleco and its ruling family."

The last bit caught Ammudien by surprise the most and incited a small amount of anger deep inside the gnome.

"What do you mean 'the shield belongs to Tyleco and its ruling family'?" Ammudien asked with a huff.

"Technically, I have a greater claim to that shield than any *human* in Tyleco," Ammudien quickly added, with a tone of rising anger.

"That shield was created for a great gnome leader and one of my ancestors. It only sat in Tyleco because some human stole it. If anything, I should take the shield and return it to Mechii, its rightful place," he said, almost shouting at Captain Cooper by the end.

Realizing the error of his words and the danger he could invite upon himself if he went against the collective opinion, Captain Cooper decided it best to calm the obviously agitated gnome. Better to be part of the group instead of against the group, he reckoned.

"I had not thought of it that way, Ammudien," Rory said calmly. "The shield had sat in Tyleco for so long that its origins had long since been forgotten. I knew it only as an heirloom of Lord Veyron's family, not a stolen treasure of the gnomes. I meant no disrespect to you or your ancestors with my suggestion, I spoke only with what I have known until now. Please forgive me and my ignorance of what was taken from your ancestors by mine."

Ammudien took several deep breaths to calm himself. Rory's apology had done much to assuage the anger that his previous statements had riled from within Ammudien, but it still took a moment for the gnome to suppress those emotions.

"I understand," Ammudien eventually said, "and I accept your apology. And I also apologize to you. My outburst was uncalled for. You did not take the shield from Mechii but have loyally guarded it all this time. In a way, I should be giving you my thanks for protecting such a treasure that might otherwise have fallen into the wrong hands."

The two shook hands in acceptance of both apologies and having gained a better perspective of the other and the sense of honor that drove them both.

"Now, I don't mean to rekindle the previous emotions," Captain Cooper started, "but I stand by my sentiment. I think we should separate the armor. Just because the greaves and shield protected Riorik from the breastplate and sword today does not mean that they can protect him from that wizard's magic or the blade of someone else in the future. Should Riorik continue to wield both pieces and should he fall in battle, then we risk losing both pieces in one fell swoop. We must do something more if we are to protect them and ourselves. The shield has found a safe home behind the sturdy walls of Tyleco for generations. There is no safer place for it than there."

Ammudien rubbed his chin as he contemplated the human's suggestion. It was a sound argument but not a foolproof one to the crafty gnome.

"I would agree that Riorik does not need to continue to bear both pieces of the armor. To that end, you and I are of the same mind. However, I must disagree that Tyleco is the best place to hold the shield."

Rory's expression was one of surprise, but before he could say anything, Ammudien continued.

"While the mighty walls of Tyleco might protect the shield, the shield was created to protect the walls. It was not meant to be stowed away to be defended but rather used to defend. The shield's ability makes it a powerful item in a fight that I feel is coming. That power will be needed on the battlefield, not locked away in an armory. I say we take the shield, or the greaves, from Riorik and give it to another member of our party. Two party members each wielding a piece of the armor makes us stronger than a party who only controls one piece. Should we encounter that wood elf and his wizard again, we will need both pieces if we are to survive."

Ammudien's idea was riskier than Rory's, but it would allow the group to maintain their current advantage as opposed to making them weaker against their probable opponent. Captain Cooper thought about both ideas and looked for the weaknesses of both before speaking. After coming to the same conclusion as Ammudien, Rory could only think of one other thing to be determined.

"So, who's going to be the one to tell Riorik that he has to give up one of the pieces?" the guard captain asked with a sly grin on his face.

Ammudien chuckled and smiled back at Captain Rory Cooper.

"I would like to say you, but I think such a request would be better coming from me," Ammudien replied.

"Do you think he will willingly accept it?" Rory asked.

"I think he will be more amenable if I explain to him that the armor would stay within the group, but if he doesn't agree, then taking it from him will certainly mean a fight I would not want to have."

"Perhaps you should conjure up one of those rock demons like what you used to capture me beforehand," Captain Cooper jokingly suggested.

"In all fairness, that's not a bad idea, but I think I'll try it first without one," Ammudien said, with a wink and a grin.

Ammudien looked over in Riorik's direction. The elf was in conversation with Nordahs and had not heard Rory and Ammudien's latest discussion. Ammudien could not help but feel a sense of trepidation and fear as he prepared to go take one piece of the armor from his friend.

Chapter 13

"So, let me get this straight. You want me to give up one piece

of the armor because you're afraid my father may kill me and take

both pieces for himself?" Riorik asked Ammudien, to make sure

he heard the gnome correctly.

"Well, I didn't use those exact words, but yes. Should

something happen to you, that would be tragic, but if in your

death, he obtained both pieces of armor in our possession, then it

would effectively doom us all. Until we know the state of his

mind and his true intentions, I think it best to divide our two

pieces among our group so that even if one piece is taken, then

we still have a chance of resisting any invasion with the help of

the remaining piece. With no armor to aid us, then there is little to

no chance of our ability to stop him if he possesses all four."

"And what piece would you have me surrender and to who?" Riorik begrudgingly asked.

"I would recommend that you pick which piece to keep and to whom you would like to give the other piece to," answered Ammudien.

Deep down, Ammudien knew that with Wuffred's death, Riorik would only pick between Ammudien and Nordahs. Captain Cooper was surely a skilled fighter given his position with the city guard, but Ammudien knew that Riorik would not entrust a newcomer to their party with such a valued prize. At the same time, Ammudien knew that if Riorik were to pick between himself and Nordahs, that Riorik would most likely choose his childhood friend over the gnome. It was much less a question of who would get the armor but more of what piece would Nordahs be given.

Meanwhile, Riorik was not surprised by Ammudien's request. The armor had been separated among the group until the battle at the oasis. Riorik also knew the significance of the shield to Ammudien. After all, the greaves that now covered his legs held a similar significance for Riorik.

"Here," said Riorik, as he thrust the shield into Ammudien's arms, "this technically belongs to you more than it does me, so it only makes sense that you become the new shield bearer of Mechii."

The gesture completely shocked the gnome. He never expected Riorik to give the armor to him. The stunned gnome just looked at the shield and stammered briefly before expressing his gratitude to his elven friend.

"Well, now that that's settled, what do we do next?" Riorik asked Ammudien.

"Actually, I was hoping you might have a suggestion," Ammudien countered.

The two discreetly talked for a few moments as they discussed different plans of action. Up until now, the plan had been for the group to recover the armor, figure out what happened to Riorik's father, and then for each of them to return to their cities with armor in hand to restore their reputations, honor, or status. Now, however, it was obvious that the other two pieces of armor were in the possession of another elf, possibly Riorik's father, and that they could not return triumphantly to their homes just yet. They had sacrificed much to get this far, so Riorik and Ammudien knew their only option was to continue forward, but neither of them knew where to continue to.

"My father was blown away from the oasis, the same as us. We landed to the south, so maybe he was thrown north. Maybe we should head north to see if we can find him or some information about his intentions," Riorik eventually suggested.

"I don't think that is wise," Ammudien quickly replied. "We would stand out among those who dwell there, and we would be severely outnumbered. We may as well just pack up the armor and deliver it to him, if that's your best suggestion."

"Well, I think we need to understand where he is headed next, if we are to plan accordingly," Riorik responded. "The armor's reaction must have knocked him away from the oasis, like it did us. Does this mean that he is now retreating to the north, is he headed west towards Nectana, is he headed south towards Kern, or is he just camped out like we are? We don't know, but if we are to find out, we have to start looking somewhere."

"That's a valid point," Ammudien conceded. "What do you say to our returning to the oasis to recover Wuffred's body so that we can give it a proper burial while we look for signs of your father's current whereabouts and potential destinations?"

"I thought you all said it wasn't safe to return to the oasis?" Riorik asked, somewhat bitterly.

"It was. It still is. But, as you said, we must start somewhere, so why not start there," the gnome answered. "Any move we make comes with a risk at this stage, so let us honor our fallen friend the best we can in that risk."

The idea of honoring Wuffred's sacrifice was very warming to Riorik's heart, so he quickly agreed with Ammudien. With the pair in agreement, they called for Nordahs and Rory to join them. Once the group was all together, Riorik laid out the plan to return to the oasis and look for signs of Cyrel's whereabouts and direction of travel, if any. The group still had not discussed if, or when, word should be sent to Asbin about Wuffred's demise. They opted to ignore that responsibility for the time being.

The only problem was that by the time Riorik regained consciousness, the various conversations among the group were had, Riorik and Ammudien agreed on their next step, and that plan was shared with the others, it had gotten late in the day. Not to mention that nobody had eaten in a while, as their thoughts had been consumed by other events. The grumbling stomachs soon drowned out the sound of voices, and one by one, the group's priorities turned to food.

"I say we enjoy a meal and get a good night's rest before setting out into the unknown," suggested Rory the guard captain.

"I agree with Rory," Nordahs said as he held his rumbling belly.

It did not take much convincing for Ammudien and Riorik to agree. The oasis would have to wait until tomorrow, but tonight, the group would eat.

***

Walking through the shifting sands, the cloaked wizard eventually topped another of the many endless dunes as he continued south towards Mechii. At the top of this dune, however, the wizard came to an abrupt stop. This dune overlooked the oasis, the location where he had found the ruins that held the breastplate of Trylon, the dwarven hero. It was also the site of their recent battle, where an elf named Riorik, who possessed the final two pieces of Ascension Armor, escaped, but not without suffering a loss of his own. The wizard looked down near the waters of the oasis where Wuffred's body could still be seen as the sands slowly began to consume him.

The wizard stood atop the dune for several minutes, looking at the destruction caused by their fight. Glass shards were scattered about from the mix of fire and sand where the wizard did battle against the tiny Terra mage. Areas of the sand were still stained with blood from where Wuffred fell after being impaled by Raiken's sword. Their camping supplies, which had been left behind when they were blown away from the oasis, laid strewn about in a twisted, tangled heap. Their abandoned gear had obviously been impacted by the same tremendous force that disrupted the skirmish.

The wizard studied the scene, trying to understand what happened. He had surmised that the events were the direct result of Raiken's sword and Sagrim's Shield clashing with one another, but he had no way to know if his assumption was correct. His time at the Mage Academy had been consumed with the study of magic to aid him in his search for the armor and his research into the whereabouts of the various pieces. The wizard had been tasked with finding the Ascension Armor for his master, not unlocking its secrets. At least, not until now.

The wizard hoped to find some clues amid the mess left behind, so he carefully descended the dune and began searching the area. His search had only begun when he heard the unmistakable sound of multiple voices approaching the oasis. Outnumbered and not looking for a fight, the wizard knew his best bet was to hide, bide his time, and search for clues later. The tall wizard quickly drew his wand and scribbled a few wispy runes that he moved from his head to his feet. As the runes passed over his body, that part of him faded away until the entire wizard was invisible to the naked eye.

Just seconds after the wizard turned invisible, Riorik and the others topped another dune before descending towards the oasis. The wizard looked from his hiding spot as Riorik and Nordahs made a direct path to Wuffred's corpse on the opposite side of the oasis. The two elves knelt around their friend's body and immediately went to work clearing the sand away that now covered parts of Wuffred. They carefully, with obvious respect, moved Wuffred's body so that he laid flat on the sandy floor on his back. The wizard continued to watch as the elves began to say what looked like prayers over the fallen human's body.

The wizard was slightly confused by what he was observing, but it was very apparent that the elves shared a great bond with the human and that they were intent on giving his death the proper respect that their traditions called for. But, it was what happened next that completely stunned the wizard.

After their prayers had been said, the two elves picked up their dead friend's body and carried it to the water's edge where their mage friend now stood. The Terra mage pointed into the water, directly towards the entrance of the ruins the wizard had found a few short days before. The elves walked into the water with the human's body and disappeared under the water's surface. A few minutes later, the pair returned, only now without their dead friend's body. The watching wizard immediately understood that they had put their friend's body in the tomb of Trylon, a place of honor.

The wizard, up to this point, had been focused on the big picture of what the group was doing and not on the individual members of the party, but it was when the elves returned to land that something grabbed the wizard's attention. The elves were ringing out their hair and clothes after their aquatic burial. One of the elves, Riorik, turned his back to the wizard's location, and the wizard noticed a scar that he recognized. It was the first time the wizard looked at the person and not the party.

"Did you hear that?" Ammudien said suddenly.

"Hear what?" Rory said, as he rushed to the gnome's side.

"It sounded like a gasp or something," the gnome said softly.

"You mean, you think we are not alone here?" the guard captain asked with obvious worry in his voice after what he had witnessed here previously.

"Wait here," Ammudien told his newest ally.

Rory did not move, just as instructed, as he watched Ammudien slowly step backward from the corner of his eye.

The tiny gnome slid behind the cover of the bigger human and into Captain Cooper's shadow. Ammudien quickly drew out a rough set of runes. The mage was more interested in speed over precision, in this case, so the sloppy runes were of little concern to him. Once the runes were complete, he readied his wand and told Rory to move to one side. Captain Cooper took a large step to the side, revealing the gnome and his runes. Ammudien wasted no time in flicking the runes across the water.

The wizard watched Ammudien send the strange runes in his direction but did not recognize the symbols with such short notice. All the hidden wizard could do was wait and watch for the runes to reveal their purpose. Unfortunately for him, the wait was brief. The runes moved to the center of the oasis before transforming into a swirling circle of smoke. With each rotation, the circle grew larger and spun faster. It did not take long for the revolving fumes to make its way to the wizard. As the magical vapors passed around him, the wizard heard a small crack as his spell was nullified, and he was once more visible to all.

"Wizard!" Ammudien yelled as he pointed to the wizard's recently revealed location.

Riorik and Nordahs quickly grabbed their weapons and spun to face in the direction Ammudien had indicated. Even Captain Cooper had drawn his sword and readied himself for combat.

"Wait!" exclaimed the wizard as he threw up his hands and stepped forward.

Only this time, the wizard's voice was not the raspy voice the group had heard earlier during the battle. Now, the voice was much more typical in sound. But more than that, the voice was one Riorik recognized.

Riorik lost his focus and dropped his sword's tip down in that moment of confusion. Riorik recognized the wizard's robes as the same clothes from the battle, but the new voice confused the young elf.

"Kirin?" Riorik asked curiously.

The wizard slowly removed his hood to reveal his face.

"Yes, it's me," came the reply from Riorik's brother, who now stood uncloaked for the entire party to see.

Nordahs now recognized Riorik's sibling also and was more stunned and confused than Riorik.

"Wait, what?" Nordahs said, as he tried to wrap his brain around this latest revelation.

But the one most shocked by this was Ammudien. The gnome was ready to fight the wizard again, but it seemed now that the wizard was a friend of his elven allies and not a foe. To a certain degree, the tiny mage felt a slight sense of betrayal.

"Did I miss something?" Ammudien asked defiantly. "This wizard tried to kill us earlier. Why aren't you returning the favor?"

Riorik turned towards Ammudien and held out his hand as if to tell the gnome to calm down and wait.

"I think that may have just been a misunderstanding," Riorik said to Ammudien, as he unsuccessfully tried to calm the mage.

"'A misunderstanding'?" a perplexed Ammudien repeated. "How could I possibly have misunderstood a giant fireball flying at my head? Then, he tried to kill me with forbidden black magic. I don't see where there could be a misunderstanding there!"

"Surely you were mistaken," replied Riorik. "My brother doesn't know any black magic, and I'm sure he wasn't trying to kill you."

Riorik turned back to Kirin. "Right, Kirin?"

Before Kirin could respond, Ammudien's temper boiled over at the situation.

"Brother?" Ammudien shouted. "That wizard is your brother? Your father tried to kill you. Your brother tried to kill me. Are there any more of your family members out there that we should know about who may try to kill us next?"

The gnome's outburst made Kirin smirk, but only briefly, as the elf quickly forced the smug grin from his lips as to not anger the short mage anymore. But he was not alone. Nordahs, too, had a small smile as he fought back a chuckle in his throat. Even Rory stood wide-eyed with his hands clasped over his mouth at Ammudien's words. It seemed the only one not entertained by the gnome's tantrum was Riorik.

Riorik took a deep breath before responding to the angry gnome.

"I understand your concern, and I don't blame you for being upset, but I would hear from my brother about why he attacked you like that before any more violence occurs. Besides, if he was helping my father, then he can tell us how to find him so we can return home."

Ammudien stared at Riorik in disbelief in the elf's naivety.

"Can I speak to you over here, alone, for a moment?" Ammudien asked his elven friend, as he motioned to an area away from the others so the two could talk privately.

As Riorik shrugged and started walking to where Ammudien had indicated. The gnome turned towards his new human ally.

"Keep a close eye on that wizard. I fear Riorik and Nordahs may be too close to this situation to be objective. If he tries anything, kill him."

The city guard captain nodded and moved closer to Kirin's position to keep watch over the elf wizard. Kirin understood the significance of Rory's approach and just held up his hands as a sign of surrender and peaceful intentions.

***

Ammudien and Riorik huddled together apart from the others to discuss Kirin's presence and intentions in a more private setting. The pair remained in view of the others but had moved to the other side of the oasis as to avoid being overheard, even by the other elves.

"Riorik, I know he's your brother and that he knows where your father is, but we have to face the facts that they did try to kill us. We can't just lower our guard and welcome Kirin into our group simply on the merits of 'he's your brother'. While I agree that your brother may have valuable information for us, we must proceed with extreme caution. I am not convinced that he can be fully trusted, despite your familial connection."

Riorik pondered Ammudien's words for a few seconds before replying.

"What would you have me do?" Riorik asked the gnome.

But, before the mage could respond, Riorik continued.

"He is my brother, and as such, I trust him with my life. He was the only friend I had for a long time before Nordahs, and he is the only other individual in all of Corsallis that knows the pain, shame, and suffering that my family has endured since my father's disappearance. I am not just going to turn my back on him now because you two exchanged some spells in an impromptu fight."

"And what of your father?" Ammudien coldly asked. "He tried to kill you. Would you welcome him with open arms too?"

"My father and I never met," Riorik retorted. "He disappeared shortly before I was born. If he tried to kill me, then it was only because he did not know who I was, only that I had the armor that he wanted. And that is why I want to talk with Kirin now. Kirin may help us to understand my father's condition so that I can return with him to Rishdel."

Ammudien reached up and placed a hand as close to Riorik's shoulder as the diminutive gnome could.

"Riorik, have you given any thought to what would happen if your father did kill his friend but was not mad?"

Riorik just looked at Ammudien with a puzzled expression. It was clear to the gnome that Riorik had never considered that as a possibility.

"Riorik," Ammudien started, "history tells us that the original bearers of the Ascension Armor lusted after the power of the other pieces, and that desire led to paranoia and seclusion. Maybe the allure of the armor was too much for a warrior like your father and he killed his friend to secure the armor for himself. From there, he was drawn to the other pieces and cannot stop until he possesses all of the armor."

"But that proves my point," countered Riorik. "If he killed Shadrack, Nordahs's father, then it was the influence of the armor and not my father that is responsible. He shouldn't be punished for something he had no control over."

Ammudien shook his head at Riorik's assertion.

"Then how come you have not killed us?" the wise gnome countered. "You have been in possession of two pieces of the armor at the same time but have not struck any of us down. You carried the greaves in your pack for days and showed no signs of aggression. So, how is it that the armor drove your father to kill his friend so suddenly after its acquisition, but you have remained so calm after all this time?"

"The madness of the protective spells," Riorik immediately answered. "He fell through the ruin's roof and broke the spell. It must have weakened his mind to the armor's influence."

"Perhaps, but perhaps not," Ammudien calmly replied.

"Look, only two elves were in the woods that day—my father and Nordahs's father. Nobody else knows for certain what transpired. That is why I must talk with my father. And that is why Kirin's cooperation is so important. Not only is he my brother, but he is also obviously working with my father, so he can lead us to him. Only then can I know the truth."

"And his involvement with the orcs and gnolls that have tried to kill us repeatedly doesn't concern you?"

"We don't know that they were working together," Riorik quickly shot back at Ammudien's suggestion. "We have only seen him in the company of Kirin. There were no orcs or gnolls at the oasis with them. For all we know, those foul beasts were looking for the armor for someone else. Maybe my father is doing the same thing we are, trying to keep the armor from falling into the wrong hands of an unknown threat, which would explain why he attacked us. He may have thought we were the malevolent force searching for the armor."

Ammudien could not argue Riorik's point. There certainly was no evidence that Kirin and Cyrel were in league with the orcs and gnolls the group had encountered so many times before. But, the lack of evidence was not proof of no connection, only that the connection cannot be proven. The intelligent gnome did not miss this fact.

"Well, I certainly can't argue that, but at the same time, we can't definitively say that you are correct either," the mage said.

"What would you suggest we do then?" Riorik asked, looking for his friend's tactical opinion.

Ammudien thought about the situation for a second before giving Riorik his recommendation.

"I agree that Kirin may have useful knowledge. However, I do not believe that he should just be accepted and welcomed as an ally, given our previous encounter. I say we nullify him as a threat and keep him under watch until we know one way or another about his intentions and the intentions of your father."

"And how do you 'nullify' a mage or a wizard?" Riorik questioned.

"That's an easy one," Ammudien answered. "We take his wand. Magic users like Kirin and myself are virtually useless without our wands. Wands are imbued with the ability to draw magic from the world around us to create the runes needed to cast our spells."

Riorik thought about Ammudien's explanation and the last Homecoming celebration in Rishdel that he spent with Kirin. The young elf remembered Kirin's firebolt and fairy fire spells but could not recall if his brother used a wand to cast them. Eventually, he had to assume that a wand must have been used but that specific detail had since been forgotten. Riorik had no reason to question Ammudien's authority on the subject.

"So that's it, then?" he asked Ammudien, expecting the gnome would have more to say about Kirin's continued presence.

"Not exactly," the gnome replied. "In addition to taking his wand, Kirin will need to be under constant supervision for the time being. I'm not convinced that he can be trusted, and as such, he should not be left alone."

"While I trust my brother," Riorik started, "I can understand your concern and would agree that we should protect everyone, even Kirin. We will accompany him in shifts. I'll take the first shift."

Riorik's offer was exactly what Ammudien figured would happen, but it was not to be.

"I'm afraid that is not exactly what I had in mind," Ammudien said.

Riorik looked down at the mage, unsure of what was meant by his last statement.

"You and Nordahs are too close to the situation. I fear that the relationship the two of you have with Kirin may cloud your judgment when it comes to him. Neither of you should be left alone with Kirin, especially you. His supervision will be split between Rory and me. This is for the protection of everyone," Ammudien explained to the confused elf.

Riorik did not appreciate Ammudien's view and countered with his own.

"Well, in that regard, you have a bone to pick with Kirin after your fight earlier. I don't think it's safe for you to be left alone with him either."

Ammudien always tried to put logic before emotion, but Riorik's words were true. The gnome mage still felt angered by Kirin's attacks and use of forbidden magic. He had to admit to himself that it would be easy for Kirin to provoke him again, even without the use of magic. Forced to admit that he was also too close to the situation to be objective at all times, Ammudien came up with another solution for Kirin's supervision.

"I'll give you that point, Riorik," the gnome admitted before continuing. "Given that neither you or I can be objective about Kirin with our various histories involving him, how about instead we do rotating shifts of pairs. You and I watch him together so that you can talk to him, but we can keep each other in check to make sure that nothing happens to us or him. Then, Nordahs and Rory can share the next shift, with each being the voice of reason to the other to prevent anyone from making a bad choice. Does that sound fair to you?"

Riorik took a moment to contemplate Ammudien's offer. He knew very little of Rory and the human's trustworthiness, but he did trust Nordahs. It did not take too long for Riorik to agree to Ammudien's terms, especially if that meant getting an opportunity to talk with Kirin about their father.

"Works for me," Riorik casually agreed, after his moment of contemplation.

With an agreement reached, the two friends returned to where the others had been left watching and wondering what had been discussed. Riorik explained the agreement to the others, while Ammudien confiscated Kirin's wand. The elven wizard did not argue and willingly handed his gnarled root of a wand to the much smaller mage.

By now, it was close to lunchtime, so the group chose to sit around together while Riorik talked with his brother to see what insights could be gained.

Chapter 14

"Tell me about Father," Riorik said, wasting no time with his brother.

"Well, I got your letter," Kirin began. "Do you remember? The one about how you talked with Mother after the Homecoming."

Riorik nodded, remembering the letter and the revelations his mother shared regarding his father's disappearance.

"I knew then what you learned. Mother tried to hide certain details from me, but I was old enough to know better. I had heard the rumors and the stories. Other elves would mock me and sling insults at me that included things that Mother tried to protect me from. I never told her what I knew, and when you asked about him, I tried to only tell you what Mother wanted me to know. So, when I got your letter, I knew that you would not sit idly by and do nothing. Your sense of pride has always been greater than mine, and you are too much like our father to do nothing when you think an injustice has been done. I knew you would search for him somehow, I just wasn't sure how."

"Yes, but what about Father? How did you find him?" Riorik interrupted.

Kirin gave a soft chuckle at the interruption.

"You still haven't changed, have you? You could never let me tell a story without trying to jump ahead," Kirin replied.

"I'm sorry," Riorik quickly apologized.

"Knowing that you would look for our father, I started my own search. I knew about the claim of him finding the Ascension Armor that '*called*' him back into the forest. Being at the Mage Academy gave me a perfect source of information to research the armor. Knowing the story of Father's disappearance and knowing you, I figured that would be the first thing you would look for. I thought that you would ask me for help, and I wanted to be ready for when that time came."

Kirin paused for a moment.

"I never imagined what I would hear next," he said in an exasperated tone. "Not long before the last Homecoming, I received a letter from Mother. She said that you had joined the Rangers Guild, to be like Father, but that you had gone missing in the forest after a mission. She said there were rumors that you had betrayed the guild, just like Father had, but the official story was that you and other Rangers had gone missing while on a scouting mission, and you were assumed dead or captured by poachers or bandits. So, you can imagine my surprise when I saw you here."

Riorik took the opportunity to tell Kirin the truth about his exit from the Rangers Guild. He explained how Wuffred, their human friend who their father had killed, was a berserker and how the guild elders had ordered him and Nordahs to kill Wuffred. Kirin's expression was one of disbelief that the elders would order such a thing, but Riorik was adamant that it was true. Riorik confessed that he could not bring himself to kill his friend, so the three agreed to flee the guild and Rishdel rather than face persecution and prosecution.

"I wanted to send word to you so you wouldn't worry, but I didn't know how without putting myself or you in danger," Riorik explained to his brother.

"But, how does this explain how you joined forces with your father?" Ammudien asked, still curious about the situation.

"Actually, it was he who found me," Kirin answered.

"I received a rather oddly stamped package at the academy one day, and when I opened it, there was a letter from my father in it. The letter said he had heard I was studying at the Mage Academy, that he wanted my help in clearing his name so he could return to Rishdel so we may all be a family again. He asked me to leave the guild and meet a friend of his because it would be too dangerous for him to come, given his outlaw status. There was an old abandoned tower west of Rhorm and southwest of Mechii, where he said his friend would be waiting for me."

"Under the cover of darkness, I left Mechii and made my way to the tower. It took me a day or two to get there without being seen, but I eventually made it. There I met a rather sketchy individual who called himself Kelig, who said he was an ally of my father and that he had information for me. I sat and listened as this Kelig person told me that my father was searching for the Ascension Armor and that it would help him prove his innocence, but he needed my help. I asked what kind of help, and he said that the tower where we met held secrets that could help locate the armor. But, he said the secrets could not be deciphered by anyone but a mage, so it would be up to me to unlock the secrets in the tower and help Father find the armor."

"At first, I thought, 'what a coincidence' because I knew you would be looking for clues about the armor too. I quickly agreed to help, thinking that it would bring us all together that much sooner. However, I knew the tower where we met, known at the academy as the Tower of Knowledge, to be forbidden. The tower was sealed shut long ago and was said to be the source of forbidden magic. I asked Kelig how I was supposed to unlock the secrets in the tower if I couldn't get into the tower. He told me that he knew a way in and showed me a secret tunnel in the nearby gold mines that was actually used as an emergency exit from the tower, when it was part of a bigger structure in the earlier ages."

"So, that's how you learned the black arts," Ammudien theorized aloud.

"Yes," admitted Kirin. "The tower held very little information about the Ascension Armor as it turned out, but there were hundreds of books and scrolls about magic from all schools, not just the forbidden one. I studied as many as I could in hopes that it might uncover something about the relics, but all it did was increase my proficiency with multiple types of magic. I spent the next few weeks going back and forth between the tower and the academy while I tried to hide my illegal activities in the forbidden structure. I received a couple of messages from Father demanding information about the armor, but I had none to give. I felt like a failure and resolved to find information on my own since the tower held none, so I set out to look for the armor. I used my detect magic skills to find an empty ruin just outside Barbos. It contained the bones of a gnome but no relic, so it would seem that you found the shield before me."

"Actually," Rory interrupted this time, "that shield has been in Tyleco's armory for generations. These three, along with the help of their friend Wuffred, stole that shield out from under my very nose. I did not know the shield's true provenance until recently and do not know how the shield came to belong to Lord Veyron and his ancestors, only that until recently it had."

"So, you did not take the shield from the tomb?" Kirin asked Riorik.

"Nope. Not us," his brother replied. "We haven't even explored that region yet."

"Then someone else must have found the tomb before me. When I got there, the tomb had already been opened. I had a look around inside, but it didn't look as if anything had been disturbed much. I figured someone had come looking for the shield, found it sitting there ripe for the taking, and they did just that."

"Perhaps the vandals belonged to your Lord Veyron's family and that's how it came to rest in your armory all these years," Kirin added, as he looked at Captain Cooper.

Kirin did not know the truth about the theft of the shield before being put into the tomb. None of them did, for that matter. The truth of the situation was that the tomb had been discovered long ago by a barbarian fighter who had been practicing his war hammer techniques nearby. During a spin attack, the hammer slipped from the fighter's hands and smashed a hole in the hidden tomb, revealing its true nature. The barbarian entered the tomb, was driven mad, and wandered off into the plains of Heilstur, never to be seen again.

Kirin then returned his attention to Riorik.

"Regardless, from there I continued north. I detected something in that direction and another to the west, but I wasn't eager to get too close to Rishdel. In all honesty, I was afraid that I might find your body after Mother's message about you going missing. I contemplated searching for you but was fearful that I would only find a corpse. That thought filled me with so much dread that I could not bear to take that chance. As long as I stayed over here, I could pretend that all was well and you were safe. That just seemed the easiest thing to do, so that's what I did. I headed north out of cowardice and fear of what I might find otherwise. Eventually, I discovered this tomb's whereabouts under the oasis, so I sent word to Father to meet me here. And shortly after his arrival, you all showed up, and from there, you know what happened next."

"So, you had contact with your father? How did you send messages to him? Where did those messages get sent?" a still suspicious Ammudien asked rapidly.

"Yes and no," answered Kirin. "I had contact with Kelig, who passed information between me and Father. I never had any direct communication with him until we met at the oasis. And to communicate with Kelig, I sent courier birds to Brennan. He said even if he wasn't there, his companions in Brennan would see that the messages were received. I would bribe merchants from nearby towns to send my messages, saying I needed to let my mother know where I was. Some resisted, but I could usually find someone willing to help. Merchants seem to be more tolerant towards other races than most people, so I used that to my advantage as often as I could."

"So," Ammudien continued, in what was now becoming an interrogation, "if you had no direct contact prior to the oasis and the only means of communication came via this third party, Kelig, then how are you certain that this individual is your father?"

"Well, the package that contained the letter instructing me to meet Kelig the first time also contained different things that I recognized from home. First, there was this pin," Kirin said, as he produced a small golden pin from his pocket.

Riorik jumped to his feet at the sight of it. It was a similar golden pin to the one he had found before joining the Rangers Guild and the same pin he noticed fastened to his father's cloak during their earlier fight. The same style of pin that he had once tried to use to barter with the postmaster of Rishdel for sending his letter to Kirin in Mechii. Riorik had carried that pin with him every day since the old elf explained its significance that day.

Riorik quickly took his pin from his pouch and held it out to show his brother.

"I found a similar pin in the forest," Riorik exclaimed.

Kirin grinned from ear to ear at his brother's find and excitement. For too long, he had assumed his little brother was dead, so to see him alive and as giddy as usual filled Kirin with joy, even if he was being interrogated by Riorik's friend.

"Yes, these pins were worn by Rangers in generations past. In more recent years, they were worn more as status symbols and decorations by veteran Rangers, like our father."

"And yours too," he added, looking at Nordahs in recognition of Shadrack's elevated position and high status among the guild and other elves of Rishdel.

"That's it? A few trinkets of elven origin? That's all it takes to convince you that some unknown individual who refuses to be seen is your father?" Ammudien asked.

"No," Kirin responded, obviously annoyed by the accusation. "Kelig offered me proof that he was helping my father by describing my mother, including her name, and by describing the interior of our childhood home in Rishdel. Nobody outside of Rishdel would have known that level of detail about my family and the inside of our home."

"Yeah, but that leaves practically every other elf in Rishdel as potential suspects," Rory added, now falling back into his role as a guard captain. "That still does little to explain how this Kelig could prove that he was working with your father and not some prankster in Rishdel."

"The package also included this," Kirin said, as he produced another item from the pockets of his robe.

Riorik's brother unfolded the leather object to reveal a piece of a leather tunic. Its design was similar to the leather tunics Riorik and Nordahs were wearing now. The key difference was across the top of the shoulder. Rangers wove bands of different colors and patterns on the shoulders of their tunics to show an individual's rank and tenure in the guild. Riorik and Nordahs had no markings on their tunics, having left the guild so soon and suddenly after being accepted as Rangers. But, the piece of leather held out before them showed the markings of a tenured Ranger captain, exactly the markings Cyrel Leafwalker would have adorned his shoulders with at the time of his disappearance.

"Still, this doesn't exactly say, 'Kirin, it's me, your father', now does it?" Rory continued with his questions.

"Well, no, but it's not like he thought, 'maybe I should take something with my name on it so one day I can prove to someone that I am who I say I am'," Kirin retorted sarcastically. "Besides, tunics like this are only given to Rangers, and it is considered extremely disrespectful for a non-Ranger to wear a tunic like this or for anyone to falsely claim a rank in the guild.

Even if this was just '*some prankster*', as you put it, even they would not go as far as to besmirch the honor and legacy of the guild in such a way. No, this is authentic. And if you look at it, you can tell that the tunic and the stitching of these rank insignias are old. This was not something made recently."

"So, when you met at the oasis, you surely recognized him then. Right?" Ammudien continued with his and Rory's interrogation of Kirin.

"Not exactly," was Kirin's answer. "He was always covered from head to toe in armor. I never saw his face. But it was his voice that confirmed it was him to me. Despite being muffled behind the mask, it was definitely a familiar voice from my childhood. There was no mistake that it was a voice that I knew but had not heard in years, not since before Riorik was born."

Still not convinced, Rory asked another question.

"And what was that initial reunion like? Did the two of you share an embrace? Talk? What?"

"Well," Kirin began, "Father always was, and apparently still is, a very focused and driven individual. He wasted no time in recovering the breastplate from the tomb upon his arrival. I did have to explain to him how the armor would expand to fit him, something I discovered in the archives in Mechii and not in the tower, but from the time he arrived at the oasis, he was all business. I'll admit that I thought that was strange and that he might express some joy in seeing his son after all these years, but considering all that's happened, I just assumed that it might have been too difficult for him and that focusing on recovering the armor was the only way he could cope with it."

Anxious to prove to Riorik that his father, and possibly Kirin, were dangerous, Ammudien asked his next question.

"And do you know to what extent your father has involved orcs and gnolls in his quest to recover the armor?"

Kirin scratched his head as he thought about the gnome's question.

"Orcs and gnolls?" Kirin replied quizzically. "I never heard anything about orcs or gnolls in my messages with Kelig. Nor were there any at the oasis prior to you all showing up."

Kirin paused a moment before continuing.

"Although, he did say something about his troops coming this way, just before he dove into the oasis to retrieve the breastplate. I didn't really get a chance to ask what troops. I just assumed they were more allies, like Kelig."

Kirin's disclosure about troops headed this way got everyone's attention. Everyone's eyes widened, and they froze in place. Instinctively, Riorik and Nordahs strained to see if their sensitive elven ears could hear anyone approaching. Riorik thought he could hear the faintest sound coming from off in the distance.

"Ammudien, go check," he worryingly said to his mage friend.

Ammudien quickly scampered away from the group and set about performing his ritual as he had so many times before. Rory was dumbfounded by what he was witnessing and asked many questions that Riorik and Nordahs casually explained the answers to. Rory now totally understood how it was that Ammudien had sensed his presence before.

Ammudien wasted no time in returning to the group as soon as his spell had ended.

"He tells the truth," were the gnome's initial words, confirming Riorik's fears. "I felt several approaching feet. Some walking, some riding, things being towed along, just a lot of various things moving this way. We should leave here. Now."

Ammudien's question about the orcs and gnolls being connected to his father had intrigued Riorik. The elf thought this to be the perfect opportunity to finally answer the question. If his father was working with the orcs and gnolls, then it stood a reasonable chance that they would be in the 'troops' headed towards the oasis. If, as Riorik believed, his father was not mixed up with that bunch, then the forces moving on their position would be absent those beasts. Riorik was determined to know which it was; now he just had to convince the others.

"Before we just turn tail and run," Riorik said, addressing the group, "I say we do some reconnaissance of our own to learn more about my father's troops—if that is who you detected, Ammudien. Perhaps these are the forces of someone else coming to take what my father protects, and he will need our help."

"I know you want answers, Riorik," replied Ammudien. "And if answers are what you seek, then just climb to the top of that dune and you will see the troops soon. But, I suggest we do not linger here long. If these troops are not friendly, they will be upon us quickly and we will be grossly outnumbered and easily overwhelmed."

Riorik needed to know. The elf could not leave without gaining every ounce of information about his father he thought possible. He led the group to the top of the dune Ammudien had indicated before. One by one, each of the party members laid down in the sand with just their heads breaching the dune's crest, and only just enough that they could see the approaching troops.

The approaching horde was nothing more than a black mass on the horizon at first, but it steadily grew bigger and bigger, a sign of the speed in which they were approaching. From their position, Riorik, with Kirin's help, found where the elf believed to be their father was waiting for the incoming troops. The elf still wore the same armor from the fight but did not have his sword in hand and ready for combat, a sign that the advancing army was his own. Now, Riorik needed to see what type of fighters made up his father's army. Was he in league with the gnolls and orcs or not? The only way to find out was to wait. And wait they did.

Ammudien was right, it did not take long for the army to arrive at Cyrel's location. And, from their vantage point, Riorik and the other elves could clearly see the variety of characters that filled the ranks of the horde below. There were dark elves and humans. A lot of them. However, in equal numbers were gnolls, orcs, and wargs. There were even a few trolls among them. This was not a friendly looking army but one that was largely comprised of the same forces that Riorik and the others had clashed with several times already.

Ammudien could not help but smirk at the confirmation of his theory. He did feel bad for Riorik though. After all, the young elf had revered his father up to this point, so the gnome knew it had to be devastating for Riorik to finally see the truth.

"We need to go," Riorik said flatly at the sight of the orcs and gnolls.

The others could hear the disappointment and pain he tried to hide in his voice. Nobody said anything in that moment. They all just dropped behind the cover of the dune before standing up and walking away. Silence ruled over the group as they just walked south. No destination or plan had been discussed, but everyone knew the goal. Riorik wanted to get far, far away.

Chapter 15

"Where are we going?" Kirin finally asked, breaking the

lingering silence that had fallen over the group.

Riorik stopped dead in his tracks at the sound of his

brother's voice. He did not know if he should be angry with Kirin

or what, considering his knowledge and involvement with their

father. The young Ranger clinched his fists closed tightly and took

a deep breath, as he tried to fight back the tears and anger that

welled up inside him. Finally, he spun around and walked straight

towards Kirin, stopping just inches from his brother's slender,

elven face.

"I'm going to get help," he said, with a wavering voice.

"Help?" Kirin asked.

"Yes, help. Our father is not the benevolent protector of

the armor that you think. Nobody nice or kind would send orcs and gnolls to slaughter dozens in the name of peace. He is corrupted by the armor, and we need to stop him before he hurts more. The killing of Nordahs's father was one death too many, but more have died because of his lust, and I will not stand idly by and watch. I wasn't around to help him before, when there may have been a chance to save our father, but that time is gone now. And, since I can't help him now either, I can at least stop him before he hurts more and brings more shame and pain to our mother."

It was obvious that Riorik's world had been shattered by what he had witnessed at the oasis. For years, his mother had told him stories about his father, about how he was a noble warrior and a hero to Rishdel. For all that time, Riorik imagined a day when his father would return home, and he would have this legendary Ranger for a father. The young elf had put his mother's memories of his father upon a very tall pedestal, and in that one instant looking over the dune's edge, that pedestal came crashing down.

"I… I-I didn't know," Kirin stuttered and stumbled as he spoke. "I wanted Father to return home too. Especially if you had gone missing as Mother's letter said. She has lost so much that I wanted to find him for her."

Kirin shared in Riorik's shock after seeing his father's affiliation with the savage forces of Narsdin. The betrayal was real for the wizard. He had betrayed the elves and the gnomes in his activities in the name of his father. Kirin felt that he was finally deserving of the shame that had been thrust upon him for so long.

"He has an army. How do we stop him?" Kirin asked, finally accepting the truth of his eyes and realizing that Riorik, and by that virtue, Ammudien too, was right.

"We get an army of our own," Riorik announced to the group.

"And where do you think this army of yours will come from?" questioned Nordahs. "You and I will certainly be branded as traitors if we return to Rishdel. Rory and Ammudien would not be welcomed there either. And Kirin, given your family standing, would likely be rebuffed as well."

Riorik considered his response briefly before answering.

"Well," Riorik started, "we have Asbin in Rhorm who can rally the dwarves. Rory here is the captain of the guard for Tyleco, so he should have some influence there. And, Ammudien can use Sagrim's Shield as leverage in Mechii. With the support of those three groups, I think we could put up a defense against Father's treachery and perhaps inspire others to come to our aid then."

Ammudien was the first to respond.

"I don't mean to 'burst your bubble', as they say, but I'm not certain that plan will work the way you suggest. Asbin is in

Rhorm, that should be true, but we cannot be certain that word will reach her in time or that she will be able to move the dwarven king to help us. And, even if she does, there is no guarantee that troops from so far away will arrive in time to be of any help to those who may soon find themselves in danger's way."

"And," Ammudien continued, "considering the terms of my departure from Mechii, I'm not so sure that I would be able to sway any gnome to come to our aid. There would be much doubt and speculation about Sagrim's Shield that they would want to validate before doing anything, and even then, the gnomes would be more likely to covet their missing relic than fight to defend those who took it from them so long ago. I would not count on the gnomes' support just yet."

Captain Cooper was the next to speak.

"I wish I had a brighter outlook than Ammudien, but I don't. I can return to Tyleco and plead with Lord Veyron to send help, but even if he agrees, the number of troops he could muster would still be much smaller than the forces we witnessed. It would take the combined forces of all the human towns to compete with that, but the lack of cooperation between them makes that unlikely without some unifying action. But, I will make haste for Tyleco and do what I can to muster what forces I can find. It's better to fight with a hundred than just five."

Ammudien and Rory's words were disheartening to Riorik, but the elf refused to admit defeat and surrender before he had even tried to do anything.

"I know this to be a difficult task, but that does not mean that we shouldn't try. Ammudien, if you accompany Rory to Tyleco, then you could send word to Asbin in Rhorm and to whoever in Mechii to warn them and ask for help. That would be faster than traveling there yourself, and there is no time to spare. Rory, once back at Tyleco, even if Lord Veyron does not agree to help, send word to the other human towns asking for help. We need everyone we can find. In the meantime, Nordahs, Kirin, and I will head to Rishdel. Even if Nordahs and I are imprisoned, then Kirin can still make our case to the guild elders there. We will need the Rangers in the fight to come."

The group fell silent as everyone thought about Riorik's plan. It was risky, very risky. It would require the group to split up and go to unfriendly territories. Ammudien, who was in possession of the shield stolen from Tyleco's armory just days before, was being asked, as a gnome, to walk into a human town—something that would be risky even if he had not helped to steal the shield. Then, the three elves, two of which abandoned their responsibilities in the Rangers Guild, were supposed to walk back through the gates of Rishdel and ask the guild leaders for help, knowing that there was a very high chance of them being killed on sight, as the sentence for their crimes against the guild was death. The one with the least to risk in this plan was Rory, but if his connection to the shield's thief was revealed, then he would most likely be considered a conspirator against Lord Veyron, which carried a sentence of death by hanging. It was a very risky plan for all involved.

Eventually, everyone agreed that it was worth the risk. The arrival of an army in the oasis at the southern edge of Narsdin could only mean one thing—an invasion of some kind. As such, if they did nothing and warned nobody, then the consequences would be severe to anyone in the advancing army's path. The army's target, or targets, were unknown, so Riorik and the others needed to warn as many people in as many towns as possible, and it only made sense to start in towns they were connected to. After years of seclusion and racial bias in all the towns and communities across Corsallis, to go elsewhere would likely raise more suspicions about themselves than anything else, and their mission would certainly fail.

Ammudien and Rory paired up and headed off to Tyleco. It was closer to their current position than Rishdel, so they would reach their destination first. Given that the two of them would have a chance to send word to others sooner than the elves, it was decided that Ammudien and Rory would send messages to all the other towns, except Rishdel, while it would be up to the Leafwalker brothers and Nordahs to warn the elves.

Riorik watched as Ammudien and Captain Cooper headed off on a different path, while he, Kirin, and Nordahs angled themselves towards Rishdel and the forest they called home. Seeing Ammudien walk away, Riorik could not help but wonder if he would ever see the gnome that he had come to call his friend again. It reminded the elf about how he watched Asbin walk away as she returned to Rhorm to give birth to her and Wuffred's child. That in turn reminded him of Wuffred's death and how his berserker friend's child would grow up never knowing his father, much like Riorik had. He sympathized with the unborn child because that was not a childhood he would have wished upon anyone.

"Don't tell Asbin about Wuffred. That should come from me," he shouted to Ammudien and Rory before they got too far away.

Riorik felt that his experiences with his own father's absence would allow him to be more sensitive to Asbin's emotions. Well, that and the fact that Ammudien was not exactly known for being anything but blunt and logical, not exactly the approach Riorik felt the situation called for. Plus, Riorik felt partially responsible for Wuffred's death. After all, it was his quest to find the armor and his father which directly led to the clash at the oasis that claimed Wuffred's life. Riorik lamented that he would not be able to tell Asbin in person about her beloved's death.

Now, all there was to do was to go their separate ways, hope that either group had some luck in convincing someone of the dangers coming their way, and that at some point, they could convince somebody to help them defend their homes against the approaching forces.

***

"What took you so long?" the armored elf furiously asked his troop's leaders upon their arrival to his location near the oasis.

"The mountain pass proved more difficult to traverse with the gear than planned," one general answered.

"And the rains that fell right before our departure slowed the wagons greatly," another said.

Having passed through the difficult mountain pass and endured the rains and floods himself should have made their leader more understanding and sympathetic to their plight, but his failure at the oasis had angered him to the point that no sympathy was to be found.

"You fools!" he shouted in contempt at his generals.

"The armor was here!" he continued. "I would have possessed the full set had you not let something as insignificant as a little water slow you down."

His words did not make sense to the generals, who looked upon their leader in his new breastplate.

"My Lord, is that not a piece of the armor there?" one general asked, as he pointed to the green breastplate and its dull blue shine in the fading light.

The dark elf general's master calmly drew the matching sword from its sheath hanging from his waist. The appearance of the blue glowing blade inspired fear among his generals. Their leader held the sword flat across his hands to show its similarity to the breastplate as he looked down at the blade's hypnotic shimmer. After a moment of retrospect, the armored elf turned around, putting his back to his generals.

"Yes, this is another piece of the ultimate armor that I have sought for so long," he said before pausing. "However, there was another here. An elf possessed the other two pieces of armor, and he challenged me for the breastplate. I succeeded in acquiring this piece but not before he managed to escape with the others. I would have had all four pieces had you not been afraid of getting wet."

As he finished his last sentence, the masked king of Macadre spun about, using the legendary sword to decapitate the dark elf. The strike was quick, and the blade's sharpness made an exceptionally clean cut clear through the general's neck. The head slowly rolled away from the slice before falling to the ground, but because of the swiftness and sharpness of the attack, it took several more seconds for the general's rigid body to fall limply to the ground.

The other generals quickly fell to the ground, groveling at their master's feet as they begged for his mercy and forgiveness for their failures. No forgiveness was spoken, as mercy was granted by the way of no other executions. Instead, the king, who remained unnamed to his subjects, just stood over his kneeling generals while he contemplated his next order.

"Rise, so that you may hear me fully as to not fail me again," he commanded the remaining generals, who quickly did as they were told.

"The plan was to march on Kern. That plan remains. Ready your troops. We leave at dawn for Kern, and it will fall before the next moon's phase," the armored elf commanded.

"And what of the elf with the other pieces of armor? Should we send troops to look for him?" another general asked, before he could think better of his actions.

His master's gaze quickly fell upon his face as the human general prepared himself for a fate similar to the last general who questioned the irritable king. No slice was felt by his throat though. Instead, his question was answered, much to his surprise and relief.

"The plan was to find or draw out the armor with our invasion. That plan holds true, only now I know who to be looking for as we raze their despicable towns to the ground. I suspect the elf will bring the armor to me in time. He and his friends seemed too noble not to defend others against our impending onslaught. And, when he reveals himself again, we will take from him by force what I was unable to secure by myself before."

"Now, go make ready for the invasion. Any more delays will not be tolerated," he declared as he dismissed his generals.

Each of the remaining generals bowed to their leader before returning to their respective regiments, anxious to see their orders completed before any wrath was directed at them.

****

It was a short march from the oasis to Kern. Ammudien and Riorik's groups were still a good way away from their destinations. Unknown to them, the invasion would begin before any warning could be issued.

As dawn broke the following morning, Macadre's king mounted his horse and prepared to lead his army of savages towards Kern and his conquest of Corsallis.

He held Raiken's sword high into the air.

"Forward," he shouted as he nudged his horse forward.

As his horse began to slowly trot, the ranks of soldiers behind followed. The plan was to arrive outside of Kern by nightfall so that when the town woke the following day, they would find themselves besieged with little hope of rescue or escape. However, the current pace was not fast enough to achieve that goal. The lead elf knew that he would need to speed up if he were to have his troops in position in time, but he needed to give the troops with the wagons and sleds a chance to move the heavy objects before speeding up, as it would be impossible for them to go from standing still to a fast pace. The physics would prevent such a rapid transition, so it required a gradual buildup of speed.

Their pace quickened as the day passed. Their orders were to march without stopping. There would be no rest and no breaks for meals. The troops would have to eat what they could find nestled in their pouches or found along the way. The desolation of the sands around the oasis meant that little would be found before reaching the irrigated farmlands outside of Kern.

Kern was built in the southern end of the dune fields that stretched from Heilstur to Narsdin. This lack of vegetation forced the humans that called Kern home to extensively work the land and dig deep, deep wells to find water for their crops, livestock, and even themselves. Water was as much a form of payment in the dry desert town as any coin. Any of the troops hoping to find food laying about were in for disappointment and hunger.

Despite the constant marching and lack of rest, the increased pace put the army back on track for reaching their destination under the cover of darkness. The army could be seen just at the horizon's edge, as the day's light began to fade and night began to take hold.

By the time the troops from Macadre came to a halt just beyond the pitiful night vision of Kern's city watch, all but the faintest of light had disappeared. The dark fur of the gnolls and dark skin of the dark elves from Nectana made them all but invisible to any prying eyes. The darker colored skin tones of the trolls and orcs helped to hide their massive frames in the absence of light. Those most visible were the paler skinned humans and the fighters who donned heavier, more reflective metallic armor. The smithed gear would occasionally glint and glimmer as different light sources would bounce off their polished surfaces.

Under the cover of darkness, the masked elf set about putting the first phase of his invasion plan into action. His plan was based on a savage deceit. He sent his stealthy gnolls around to the south of the city, where they were to hide and wait. His dark elf archers were sent to the west of the city, the likeliest path for any birds trying to carry messages to other cities, with instructions to shoot down any courier birds trying to enter or exit the city. To the east of the city, he positioned his wargs and warg riders. Nothing but the coast laid east of Kern. but just in case anyone tried to escape in that direction, his fast running wargs could run them down with ease. The rest of his troops remained with him, north of the city, in direct sight of the city's main entrance. This would be his plan's masterstroke, leaving his armored forces and oversized orcs and trolls in plain sight for the city's inhabitants.

When the sun rose, he would demand the city's surrender or destruction. With the dark elves and gnolls in hiding, there would undoubtedly be attempts to send requests for help to other cities, and several people would likely attempt to flee through the southern gate. His archers would ensure that no help could be called, and his gnolls would descend upon the unsuspecting citizens attempting to escape. As the others saw their friends, families, and neighbors being torn to shreds by the gnolls with their frenzied attacks, the mad elven king was certain that they would run back to the safety of the city. Surrounded, unable to escape, unable to seek help from others, the city would have no option but to surrender in the face of such overwhelming numbers and brutality.

Kern was expected to fall quickly, giving the invading army a more permanent and fortified position to stage their future attacks. Plus, an invading force would require sustenance. The stockpiles of grain and meats would help refill the depleted supplies of the forces who saw a rushed departure from Macadre.

However, Kern's less fruitful surroundings meant that it would yield fewer goods than other cities, so the plan was always to advance and occupy the other cities that dotted the lands to be conquered.

With his orders issued and his troops moving into position, there was little left to do but wait until morning. The elven king did wonder about his wizard and his whereabouts. The thought had crossed his mind that his wizard may have stopped here on his way back to Mechii, but that was a risk the masked king was willing to take. He was not planning to have to take Kern by force, so even if his wizard was behind Kern's walls, he should still be safe from harm from the invading force.

Eventually, the night began to give way to the light of day once more. The first ray of light marked the onset of the invasion and conquest of Corsallis.